"Mr.

He looked down at the piece of paper in his hand—the list of questions his sister-in-law had helped him come up with—and shook his head. "Gail thinks you'll make the perfect nanny for Will."

"But you're not so sure," she said shrewdly.

Faith McClain was perceptive. He smiled.

"No, you'll do fine—it's me I'm worried about."

Dear Reader,

Over the past few years a number of readers have asked me when I was going to write Brian Kincaid's story. Since the last Kincaid brother was as much a mystery to me as to my readers, I couldn't have said. Then, a few months ago, when I was supposed to be working on another book, it occurred to me to ask what was the worst thing that could happen to man like Brian Kincaid. World traveler, fun-loving, eternal bachelor Brian could never see himself settling down.

Until he became an instant father. Trying to parent motherless child he'd never even known he had wa difficult for Brian, to say the least. Hiring suddenly unemployed Faith McClain to help him seemed lik the answer to his prayers. Faith was plain and sweet not the sort of woman to tempt him. Or so he thought until he began living with her, his son and Faith's baby girl. He'd never imagined falling for al three of them....

Faith knows Brian Kincaid's type. Charming and irresponsible, just like the man who walked out on her and her baby. But Faith soon learns not to judg Brian by his past. And she realizes that she could b in a lot of trouble, falling for the one man she can' have.

I hope you enjoy Brian and Faith's journey. I love to hear from readers. Write me at P.O. Box 131704, Tyler, TX 75713-1704 or e-mail eve@evegaddy.net and visit my Web site at www.evegaddy.net.

Eve

SS

WASHOE COUNTY LIBRARY

3 1235 03347 8111

THE ... BABY

DATE DUE

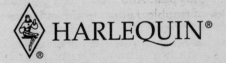

HARLEQUIN®

TORONTO • NEW YORK • LONDON
AMSTERDAM • PARIS • SYDNEY • HAMBURG
STOCKHOLM • ATHENS • TOKYO • MILAN • MADRID
PRAGUE • WARSAW • BUDAPEST • AUCKLAND

If you purchased this book without a cover you should be aware that this book is stolen property. It was reported as "unsold and destroyed" to the publisher, and neither the author nor the publisher has received any payment for this "stripped book."

ISBN-13: 978-0-373-71457-5
ISBN-10:   0-373-71457-2

THE CHRISTMAS BABY

Copyright © 2007 by Eve Gaddy.

All rights reserved. Except for use in any review, the reproduction or utilization of this work in whole or in part in any form by any electronic, mechanical or other means, now known or hereafter invented, including xerography, photocopying and recording, or in any information storage or retrieval system, is forbidden without the written permission of the publisher, Harlequin Enterprises Limited, 225 Duncan Mill Road, Don Mills, Ontario, Canada M3B 3K9.

This is a work of fiction. Names, characters, places and incidents are either the product of the author's imagination or are used fictitiously, and any resemblance to actual persons, living or dead, business establishments, events or locales is entirely coincidental.

This edition published by arrangement with Harlequin Books S.A.

® and TM are trademarks of the publisher. Trademarks indicated with ® are registered in the United States Patent and Trademark Office, the Canadian Trade Marks Office and in other countries.

www.eHarlequin.com

Printed in U.S.A.

ABOUT THE AUTHOR

Eve Gaddy is an award-winning author of more than fifteen novels. She lives in east Texas with her husband and her incredibly spoiled golden retriever, Maverick, who is convinced he's her third child. She is currently hard at work writing more Superromance novels.

Books by Eve Gaddy

HARLEQUIN SUPERROMANCE

Don't miss any of our special offers. Write to us at the following address for information on our newest releases.

Harlequin Reader Service
U.S.: 3010 Walden Ave., P.O. Box 1325, Buffalo, NY 14269
Canadian: P.O. Box 609, Fort Erie, Ont. L2A 5X3

This book is in memory
of my mother-in-law, Peggy Gaddy, who gave me
love and understanding for more than thirty years,
and who shared her wonderful son with me.
I miss you, Peggy.

CHAPTER ONE

BRIAN KINCAID didn't much like lawyers. Especially not the kind who'd track him down while he was with a beautiful brunette. And the kind who'd insist on meeting with him without telling him why *really* yanked his chain. But Brian knew lawyers. So he figured it would be easier to agree to see the guy than to try to put him off.

That didn't mean he was happy about it. In fact, he was in a pretty poor mood by the time he arrived at the address the lawyer had given him. Obviously, he thought, eyeing the weathered building near downtown Dallas, this wasn't one of the more successful attorneys. Unless he was just cheap.

"Thank you for coming," Harry Riffkin said, showing Brian into a cramped office that had seen better days.

"You didn't give me much choice. What's all the mystery about?" He refused the offered chair, hoping the man got the point that he was in a hurry.

He had a lunch date with a blonde he'd met the night he flew back from China, three days ago.

"Sorry about that, but this kind of news is best given in person." Instead of telling him, though, the lawyer sat, steepled his fingers and looked pensive. Annoyed, Brian decided to take a seat after all. "Do you recall a woman named Adrianna Shipley?"

Brian shook his head. He remembered faces. He didn't do as well with names. "I need a little more information."

"She was a flight attendant for American Airlines. That's where you met. You had a relationship with her nineteen months ago."

Nineteen months ago? He counted back. "Yeah, I remember her. Blond, short." And built. Really built. "Talked a lot." He now remembered she'd been amazing in bed, too. But he couldn't recall much else about her. "I wouldn't exactly classify what we had as a relationship. We saw each other only a few times." It had been fun while it lasted but neither of them had wanted anything serious. The women he dated rarely did and that was just the way he liked it.

"You saw her enough times to father her son," the lawyer said drily.

His stomach sank. Then anger kicked in. "So that's what this is about. A paternity scam. How gullible do I look to you?"

"Ms. Shipley has named you as her ten-month-old son's father. Are you denying paternity?"

"Hell, yes." Brian stood and paced the small room. "I know damn well we used protection. She's lying. The question is, why'd she wait so long? Did her alternate plan fall through?"

"Are you telling me it's impossible that you're the father of her child?"

He started to say just that but hesitated. "I'm saying it's unlikely. Does she want money, is that it?"

Riffkin shook his head. "No, not money." He paused. "Adrianna Shipley is dead. She died in a car accident five days ago. According to her will, you're her son's only living relative." He leaned his forearms on the desk and pinned Brian with a surprisingly stern look. "What she wanted, Mr. Kincaid, was for you to take responsibility for your son. Your now motherless son."

Brian had a bad feeling. A very bad feeling. Condoms weren't foolproof. And he'd definitely had sex with Adrianna. But...footloose Brian Kincaid, world traveler, a father? Stunned, he sank back into the chair.

"I know it's a shock, but there's a simple way to prove—or disprove—Ms. Shipley's claim. Anticipating you would want proof, I contacted a DNA lab. They already have a sample from the child. I was told we can have the results by day after tomorrow if you go down there today."

Brian's head was spinning. *Hello, Daddy.* No, he couldn't be a father. Could he? "All right. I'll take the test." What choice did he have? "Where's the kid now?"

"He's with a friend of his mother's, Kara Long. I have a letter that was to be given to you in the event of Ms. Shipley's death." He picked up a sealed envelope and handed it to Brian. "She also left one for Mrs. Long, detailing her wishes regarding her son. I'm sure she'll be happy to share it with you in the event your paternity is proved."

Brian took the envelope and stared at it a moment, then ripped it open.

Brian,
It's true. All you have to do is look at him to know he's yours. Take good care of him and tell him his mother loved him.
Adrianna

He turned it over but that was it. Three lines? Three lousy lines to drop this bombshell? "That's it? That's all she left for me?"

"It's all I was given. There may be more information, records and such, among her belongings.

It's not unusual that she left little with me. Most people don't expect to die at her age."

"She thought about it enough to leave me a letter. And to contact a lawyer."

Riffkin spread his hands. "A precaution, merely, to protect her child."

"She should have told me."

"I agree. However, she didn't. And you're a hard man to get a hold of, Mr. Kincaid. It's taken me a few days to track you down."

"I've been working overseas."

"Yes, it's fortunate you came back to the States when you did."

Fortunate for who? Brian wondered.

Riffkin tapped his fingers on the desk. "Uh, I get the impression Mrs. Long would like to get this matter taken care of as soon as possible."

"That makes two of us," Brian said, standing. "Where's this DNA lab?"

Riffkin handed him a piece of paper with two addresses on it. "The top one is the lab. The one below it is Mrs. Long's address, in case you'd like to see the child. She lives in the same apartment complex Ms. Shipley lived in."

Brian didn't answer, just took the paper and left. Seeing the child would make this…experience… even more surreal than it already was. On the other hand, he wouldn't get the results for two days. If the baby looked nothing like him he might sleep easier. One way to find out.

BRIAN HEARD CHILDREN shrieking, a woman hollering and a TV blaring in the background. None of that freaked him out. His brother Mark's house always sounded like a riot was going on in it. His brother Jay's place wasn't much better. Each of them had three kids of varying ages and kids were not quiet. That was only one of the reasons he was glad he didn't have any. He liked peace and quiet.

Yeah, and what are you gonna do if this kid is yours? If you're a dad? He shook his head to clear the thought and knocked.

He had to pound on the door three times before it was answered. "Well, well." A clearly exhausted woman leaned against the doorjamb and looked him up and down. "You must be Brian Kincaid."

"That's right. How did you know?"

"The lawyer gave me a heads-up. And you fit Adrianna's description. Tall, dark and too damn good-looking to be for real."

He smiled at that. He was beginning to remember more about Adrianna. She'd had a smart mouth. "Thanks."

"She didn't mean it as a compliment." Leaving the door open, Mrs. Long turned away. "I'll get his things."

"Wait a minute. I don't even know if he's my kid. I just came to—"

She interrupted him. "Are you going to take him or not? I need to know because if you aren't, I'm calling Child Protective Services today. I have four kids of my own under the age of six and a husband who thinks helping with child care means taking out the trash."

"You can't seriously expect me to take a kid I don't even know for sure is mine."

"You or CPS," she said adamantly. "Look, I didn't even know Adrianna that well. When I said I'd do this, I never expected her to die and I sure as hell didn't sign up to be her baby's permanent guardian."

Foster care. That's where he and Jay would have ended up if Mark hadn't taken them in when their mother had dumped them. No son of his—if this *was* his son—was spending any time in foster care.

"I'll take him," Brian said.

SHE'D NAMED HIM WILLIAM but had called him Will. The birth certificate said Brian Kincaid was the father. But Adrianna hadn't made a single attempt to let him know he was a dad. Not once. After they'd been together that handful of times, she hadn't called him again. But then, what she knew about Brian probably didn't make her think of him as prime father material. His job as a computer specialist—a troubleshooter for computer security systems for large companies—took him all over the world. Not to mention he was always sure to make it clear that he was not into serious relationships. Never had been, never would be.

But now he had to figure out how to take care of a ten-month-old for at least two days. Once she'd been assured he would take Will, Kara Long had been helpful. Sort of. When pressed, she'd shown him how to change a diaper and told him how and what to feed the baby. She said Adrianna would have everything he needed at her place. Then she gave him a key to Adrianna's apartment and told him to make himself at home. Brian had to make two trips from Kara's to Adrianna's, struggling with a car seat and more crap than he had ever hauled around for any of his trips, before he could come back for the kid. Finally, he went back for the baby and fought down a feeling of panic when Kara handed Will to him.

"Don't worry. One is nothing. Try dealing with two-year-old twins and a four- and five-year-old." Then she shut the door in his face.

Will promptly started to cry. *Oh, shit*, Brian thought. *What am I supposed to do now?*

HALF AN HOUR LATER, Will was still screaming. It then dawned on Brian that the boy might be hungry so he took him into the kitchen and put him in his high chair, which seemed to please him since he quieted down. Brian searched the cupboards and found some baby cereal as well as some formula and jars of other food. He made up some cereal and picked out a jar of carrots, found a spoon—a small one he assumed was for the baby—and sat down.

"We're cooking with gas now," he told Will and dipped the spoon into the jar.

Will blinked big, wet green eyes at him and stuck his fingers in his mouth. Brian offered him the carrots but he wouldn't remove his fingers. He tried the cereal and that was marginally better—Will finally did pull his fingers out of his mouth, though when he did, he stuck them in the cereal bowl and flung globs of the stuff around. Eventually, Brian got him to eat some, but by the time he'd gotten halfway through the jar, Will, Brian and part of the kitchen were all wearing orange and gray. Giving up on the vegetables, Brian found some kind of sausages in a jar. Maybe the kid wanted meat, he thought.

He didn't eat it, but he seemed to enjoy smashing it into the high-chair tray and then threw it on the floor. Brian understood now why you bathed a kid after dinner and not before. After a good half hour of watching Will launch food everywhere, Brian decided he must not be hungry. Kara had said to give him a bottle before bedtime, so he figured if he did that, the kid wouldn't starve.

Not knowing anything about it, Brian didn't feel comfortable bathing the baby. He decided he'd do research before he tried that. Surely he could find some information on the Internet. Four hours later Brian crept out of Will's room, praying he wouldn't wake. He'd managed to wipe him off and get him more or less clean and change him into his pajamas. The kid had sobbed his heart out and screamed for his mama until he'd finally fallen asleep from pure exhaustion. Brian wasn't sure what he'd do if the baby woke again.

But for now the kid was asleep and he needed to take advantage of that. He found Adrianna's laptop and booted it up. People took care of babies every day. It couldn't be that hard, could it? Especially if he could read up on it. He typed in "how to take care of a ten-month-old baby" and started reading. An hour later his head was spinning. Too much information and in no particular order, he thought. Maybe Adrianna had some books that would help him out. He went to her bedroom and found *What To Expect: The First Year*, took it with him to the den and got comfortable. He realized after only a few pages that the book was exactly what he needed.

Finally, when he couldn't take in any more information, he went back to Adrianna's room and climbed into her bed. He felt kind of weird about that but decided it was stupid to let a perfectly good bed go to waste. Besides, her couch was so short he couldn't stretch out on it. Hours later, he woke from a deep sleep and wondered where he was. Not in his apartment, that was for sure.

Then he heard it. "Mama, Mama," Will sobbed. It all came back to him in a rush. He had a son. Maybe. But it didn't matter whose kid he was, Brian had to go to the child. He couldn't let him cry alone, although he suspected nothing he did would satisfy the little boy. He wanted his mama and his mama wasn't coming back. Ever.

Brian knew what that felt like. Exactly. Only he'd been eleven when his mother had walked out of his life. And while his own tears had been mostly silent, he could empathize with the pain behind Will's heartbroken sobs. He wondered if Will would learn, as he had, that it was far better not to love than to risk having someone you love and depend on leave you. And in doing so, trample your heart into tiny pieces.

Brian trudged into the baby's room and picked him up. He tried to cuddle him but the kid wasn't having any of it. His arms and legs went rigid and he screamed "Mama" at the top of his lungs.

"Sorry, Will," he murmured. "You're stuck with me." At least Brian had been left with his brothers. Poor Will only had him, a total stranger who might, or might not, be his father.

CHAPTER TWO

Faith McClain squinted, trying to decipher the scrawl on the paper in front of her. *Bolos*? Wasn't that Spanish? No, she decided, the word was *books*. It was really unfortunate that one of the most prolific clients for the secretarial service her office provided had such lousy handwriting. And unfortunate that she had to be the one to transcribe it.

Along with secretarial help, the leasing office of the high-rise University Tower building in Corpus Christi, Texas, offered an answering service for its tenants. Thankfully, the lines weren't usually very busy, but today the phones had been ringing nonstop.

Faith stifled a yawn as she reached for her coffee mug, forgetting it was empty. Her baby, Lily, had been fussy the night before and Faith was running on about four hours sleep. Maybe another cup of coffee would fix her up, she thought. No, that would just make her more wired.

The phone rang again and she picked it up. "University Tower. Faith McClain speaking. How may I help you?"

"Ms. McClain, this is Jane from Noah's Ark Day Care. You need to come pick up Lily. She's running a temperature of a hundred and two."

Again. Faith's heart sank. She'd already taken a day off this week because her baby was sick. But she'd thought it was just a cold. Lily had seemed well enough to go back to day care. "I'll be there as soon as I can."

She hung up, sucked in a breath and squared her shoulders, prepared to face her boss, Stephanie Lawson. Stephanie wasn't a bad boss, just a little impatient. And the pay was decent, even if she did have to commute to Corpus Christi from nearby Aransas City. It would be easier if she moved to Corpus, but she couldn't afford it. She'd rather raise Lily in a smaller town, anyway.

No, the real problem was that Faith was a single mother and had no one else in the world to depend on. Stephanie had warned her earlier in the week that she wasn't happy about all the time off Faith seemed to need. Lily had had a string of illnesses ever since she'd gone into day care. The center tried, but sick kids were a fact of life.

Faith tapped on the door and entered. Her boss looked up and smiled. "Can you show a client one of the vacant offices around one? I'm trying to get these bank deposits finished and don't want to take the time."

Her face must have given her away. "Not again. What is it now?" Stephanie asked, frowning.

"The day care called. I have to go pick up Lily." She pushed her glasses back up her nose and waited for the reaction. She had a feeling it wouldn't be good.

Stephanie tapped her pen, then went back to the checks spread over her desk. "We discussed this earlier this week. I've got far too much work to do today to have you going off the clock."

The leasing office was busy, especially with the secretarial and answering services, so Stephanie's complaint wasn't entirely unjustified. "I'm sorry. I could take some work home with me and bring it back tomorrow."

"No, *I'm* sorry." She laid down her pen and looked at Faith. "I need you here, not at home. This isn't working, Faith. I need someone I can depend on. Not someone who takes off every other day."

"Lily's day care won't keep her if she's running a fever. I don't have a choice." Her stomach hurt. She needed the job. If she was fired she wasn't sure that unemployment would cover her rent. Not if she was going to buy food, too.

Stephanie pushed her chair away from the desk. "I don't have a choice, either. I'm afraid I'm going to have to let you go."

"You can't give me another chance?" She hated to beg, but for Lily's sake, she'd do it.

Stephanie shook her head. "I've given you a number of chances. Nothing's going to change, Faith. Not when your child is ill so often."

She knew her boss's mind was made up. She'd seen this coming, after all. "All right. I'll get my things."

Stephanie followed her into the outer office. "You'll receive severance pay and unemployment. You'll be all right, I'm sure. I'll give you a good reference. When you're here you do your work very well."

"Thank you." Faith started gathering the few personal items she had there. The job hadn't been her favorite, but it had been far from the worst. And it had paid the bills. "Do you need me to work until you find my replacement? After Lily can go back to day care, I mean."

"No, I'll get a temp."

"All right. I'll be in touch about that reference. And I'll take Mr. Tyson's work home and finish it. I'll drop it by tomorrow."

"Thanks, I appreciate that. Good luck, Faith."

She'd need it. She picked up her things and walked out the door.

Forty-five minutes later, she sat in Dr. Jay Kincaid's examining room with Lily. Luckily, his nurse had managed to squeeze them in, and the doctor walked in shortly after they arrived.

"What seems to be the problem?" Dr. Kincaid asked as he washed his hands. He had to speak loudly to be heard over Lily, who was crying as if her heart were broken. Faith smoothed her hair, wishing she could help.

"I think she has another ear infection. I kept her home earlier this week but I thought she just had a cold."

"Hello, beautiful," he said to the baby. "You get prettier every time I see you." He began the examination and Lily quieted almost immediately, kicking her feet and waving her chubby hands.

Faith figured he said that to all his young patients, but with Lily's blond curls and big blue eyes, Faith agreed she was a striking baby. Unfortunately, her own hair wasn't nearly as pretty as her daughter's, being more mousy dishwater than golden-blond. And it needed a cut so badly she probably looked like a poorly groomed poodle.

Unlike the man taking care of her child. Tall, blond and handsome, she knew a lot of women in town were disappointed that he was so devoted to his wife and family. "I wish I had your magic. Do they always quit crying for you?"

He chuckled. "No way. And my own son has a set of pipes you wouldn't believe."

Along with two older stepdaughters, Dr. Kincaid had a fourteen-month-old son. "How are your wife and kids?" Faith knew them slightly, since they went to the same church. She had only moved to Aransas City from Corpus Christi after Lily's birth. Faith's roommate had suddenly decided to get married and move out. She'd had to find a cheaper place to live quickly. Aransas City was close by and the housing was cheaper.

"They're good. Thanks for asking." He looked in Lily's throat, listened to her chest and checked her ears.

"She's only six months old. Is it normal for her to be sick so much?" Faith couldn't remember how many times they'd been in Dr. Kincaid's office in the past few months.

"One of the hazards of day care," the doctor said, putting down his otoscope. "Your diagnosis was right. Lily has an ear infection. I'll give you a prescription for an antibiotic. Don't let her go back to day care until she's been fever free for a full day. Will that be a problem?" He pulled a prescription pad out of his pocket and began to write.

Dr. Kincaid knew all about her situation. "Not anymore. I lost my job today."

He tore the sheet off the pad and handed it to her. "I'm sorry, Faith."

"Me, too." She sighed, determined to think positively. "I need another job. Have you heard about anything around here? If I didn't have to commute, it would be great."

"No, but I'll let you know if I do." He washed his hands and added, "The holidays will be here before too long. Maybe there will be some seasonal work over Christmas. Although a lot of that will be in Corpus."

She nodded. "I'll look into that if I don't find something here." Not that she held much hope, but at least she could try. "Thanks for everything, Dr. Kincaid."

"YOU DON'T KNOW of any job openings around here, do you?" Jay asked his wife, Gail, when he arrived home. He stopped and sniffed as he tossed his keys on the kitchen counter. An unidentifiable smell filled the air. Not exactly a bad odor but not good, either.

"No. Why?" Gail pulled a casserole out of the oven and wrinkled her nose. "I think I forgot one of the ingredients. It's supposed to be fluffy." She turned to her husband. "Does this look fluffy to you?"

It was as flat as a tortilla but he didn't say that. He laughed. "I didn't marry you for your cooking abilities." He turned her around and took her in his arms. "But your kissing abilities are phenomenal."

Gail returned his kiss before looking up at him and arching a brow. "Flatterer. But I'm better at cooking than I used to be."

Jay didn't answer, just kissed her again.

"Oh, Jason must have heard you come in," Gail said as the voice chanting *Daddy* interrupted them from the other room. "Will you go get him? He's in his playpen in the den."

"Absolutely." When he returned holding their son, he told her, "Faith McClain needs work. Her baby is sick again and she lost her job. She was a secretary in a leasing office in Corpus Christi."

"Oh, that's too bad. I know what it's like to be a single mom, but at least I had my family. I don't think she has a soul who can help her. She just can't catch a break, can she?"

"Apparently not. I'll ask around and see if anyone knows of any openings. I don't think she's picky."

"My real estate office might have something. It won't hurt to ask."

The phone rang and Jay picked up. "Hello."

"You've got to help me. I swear, Jay, I don't have a clue how to do this."

"Brian?" Jay didn't think he'd ever heard his brother sound so frantic. "What's going on? I can hardly hear you."

"He won't stop crying. I've tried everything. At least, everything I could think of. He just keeps screaming."

"Who? That sounds like a baby. Are you at one of your girlfriends' houses?" Surely someone hadn't left Brian alone with an infant. He was fine with older kids but knew nothing about babies.

"Don't I wish. No, the baby you hear screaming bloody murder? He's my son."

CHAPTER THREE

"I PUT WILL in the playpen you brought with you, but tomorrow I'll see if we can borrow a crib. He's down for the count," Gail said, coming back into the living room. "The poor little guy is totally exhausted." She looked at Brian as if expecting a comment.

"You'd be exhausted, too, if you'd screamed your head off for most of the last nine hours." He'd never thought of himself as a nervous person, but every nerve he had was totally shot. He held out his hand, surprised it wasn't shaking.

"It's only a seven-hour drive from Dallas," Jay said.

"Not when you've got a crying baby in the car and you have to stop every ten minutes to change him or feed him or whatever." He mulled that over. Maybe the kid was sick. "Is it normal for a baby to cry so much? You should look him over again, Jay. I think he's got something wrong with him."

Gail laughed and took their son from Jay. "He's teething, Brian. And he's got diaper rash. Jason would be crying, too, in that situation." She glanced at her watch. "Speaking of Jason, I'm going to give him a bath before Mel and Roxy get home from dance class. Their father is dropping them off in about an hour."

Brian rubbed his temples. Who knew diaper rash was such a big deal? "I put that white crap on him. It's supposed to clear it up."

His brother stared at him. "How did you know that? As far as I know, you've never changed a diaper in your life. You sure as hell never changed one of Mark's or my kids."

Brian lifted a shoulder. "I read about it on the Internet."

"That's kind of scary," Jay said chuckling. "Everything I needed to know about child care I learned on the Internet."

"You wouldn't think it was so damn funny if you were an instant dad," Brian said sourly. "I think I've aged ten years in the last three days."

"I'm not laughing. Much. But seriously, how sure are you that you're the father? I mean, you said she never even mentioned being pregnant to you."

"I'm sure. I've got the paternity test results to prove it. Besides, he looks like me."

"Yeah, he does. Except you had blond hair as a kid and his is dark like yours is now."

"Whatever, other than hair color, he's a carbon copy of me as a kid."

"So, what are you going to do?"

"I don't know." He took a sip of beer. He'd hardly had a chance to think since he'd found out about Will. These past few days he'd felt as if he'd been struggling not to drown. Not conducive to big decision making. "My job…it's the perfect job for a single guy. But for a father? How am I supposed to take care of a kid when they send me to China? Or London? Or Argentina?"

"Good point." Jay was silent for a moment. "I thought you were back in the States for good?"

"Yeah, so did I but my boss changed his mind. He keeps saying it's just one more assignment, but I'm not counting on that."

"You could quit the job. Start your own business. You've said before you'd considered doing that."

Yeah, he'd thought about starting a computer troubleshooting and consulting business, but he'd wanted to do it in his own time, not be forced into it.

"Or you could give Will up for adoption," Jay continued.

Brian stared at him. "What part of 'this is my kid' did you not understand? I'm not giving him away to strangers."

"Technically, you're a stranger, too."

Through no fault of his own. And that grated. "I'm his father. He's my responsibility."

"I figured you'd say that, but I thought I'd ask."

"He's already lost his mother." Brian shut his eyes, trying not to remember the haunting cries of "Mama" that he'd been hearing since he picked Will up from Kara Long's. "I'm not giving him away and I'm sure as hell not dumping him in the system."

"Okay, okay," Jay said. "I just said it's an option."

"Not for me. What am I going to do?" He got up and paced. "I don't know how to take care of a kid. It's a miracle he survived the past few days."

"Don't be so hard on yourself. You did okay. Babies are difficult. Especially when you're new at it. If it weren't for Gail, I wouldn't have had a clue what to do with Jason."

Brian shook his head. He'd never felt so incompetent in his life and he sure as hell didn't like it. Give him a computer any day. They might be frustrating at times, but he knew what to do with one. Besides, worst came to worst, you could always reformat the sucker's hard drive and start over. You couldn't do that with a baby.

"If you're worried about finances, I can help you out. It's going to take time to get your business off the ground—if you decide to start your own, that is."

Brian smiled at his brother. "Thanks, but money's one thing I don't have to worry about. I've had a great-paying job since I got out of school and no one but myself to spend the money on."

Gail came back in with Jason and handed him to Jay. "He wants to kiss Daddy good-night."

Brian watched the three of them. They looked so calm. So happy. So together. They were a family, along with Gail's daughters, Roxy and Mel. You sure couldn't say that for him and Will. But he needed to think of practicalities. "I can't take care of him alone. I've got to have help, and a place to live. We obviously can't stay here forever." Mel had given up her bedroom for Brian and Will, which was fine for a few nights, but not long-term.

"You're not going back to Dallas? What about your job?" Gail asked him.

"I'll have to go back to arrange to move both Will's stuff and mine, but no, I don't think I'll stay there. Most of the family is here. Even Mom and Walt aren't in Dallas much anymore," he said. His mother and her second husband traveled often these days. "If I'm going to start my own business, it might as well be down here."

It wouldn't be all bad. He'd get to spend time with his brothers and their sister, who'd found them recently after a twentysomething-year absence. Miranda, or Ava as she now called herself, had married Mark's next-door neighbor and was living in Aransas City, too.

He'd never imagined settling in a small town, though. Why would he when he'd lived all his life in Dallas and a series of exotic locations? But he hadn't had a child to consider then.

"I think moving here's a great idea," Gail said. "And I can help you out with finding a place to live. A family in our neighborhood was recently transferred and had to move unexpectedly. The house just went on the market. If you like it and want to buy it, I'm sure they'd be open to you renting it until you could set the closing date."

He rubbed his neck and scowled. "What's the catch? Is it ugly? Or needs a lot of work?"

Gail laughed. "No, it's a perfectly nice house. And big. I guess you're just lucky."

He didn't feel so lucky. But he knew better than to say that aloud. "Thanks. Can you get me in to see it?"

"First thing tomorrow," she promised. "As for Will, you don't just need help, Brian. You need a nanny."

"A nanny?" He stopped when he noticed that Jay and Gail were looking at each other as if they'd just discovered fire. "You mean, someone to live with us? Why can't I just put him in day care?"

"Because you don't know jack about taking care of a kid," his brother said with brutal honesty. "Child care isn't the only thing to worry about, either. You've got to make a home for him, Brian. And you'll probably have to work some irregular hours if you're starting a new business. Having a nanny just makes sense."

True on all counts. "So now I have to interview potential nannies? Great. How the hell am I supposed to do that? I don't know anything about hiring a nanny."

"Don't worry about that. We know just the person to help you out."

"Faith McClain," Gail said, turning to him enthusiastically. "Oh, Brian, she'll be perfect. Tell Brian about her and I'll be right back," she said to Jay and left to put the baby to bed.

"So who is this 'perfect' nanny?"

"One of my patients. She's a single mother who just lost her job. I think she'll jump at the chance. It would mean she wouldn't have to put Lily in day care anymore."

"A single mother? With a baby?" Another baby? He wasn't used to *one* yet. Not good. Not good at all.

"Yeah. She has a six-month-old little girl."

Brian sat down. It was that or fall down. He stared at Jay incredulously. "You want me to live with a woman I've never met before, my ten-month-old son I met for the first time just three days ago and a six-month-old baby? Are you out of your ever-lovin' mind?"

TWO DAYS LATER, Brian knew he was the one who'd lost his mind. Jay, Gail and all their kids had given him the run of the house so he could interview in peace, but he had a cowardly urge to call Gail and beg her to handle the whole thing. He resisted, in part because he knew Gail wouldn't do it. Though she had helped him with Will, she had also made it clear that Brian needed to learn how to take care of his son by himself. Which meant that he, not his sister-in-law, would be the one to hire the new nanny.

Faith McClain showed up on time with baby in tow. She perched on the couch, a cloth over her shoulder and her baby positioned over it. Apparently Faith hadn't been wearing the cloth earlier, Brian noticed, because there was a big stain of something yellow—he didn't want to know what—on her other shoulder.

He'd taken her in to see Will right away. As far as he could tell, Will liked her, but then the kid seemed to like all women. Just like his dad, Brian thought, hiding a smile. Faith carried both babies into the other room while he carried the playpen. If they let Will explore like he wanted to they'd never get finished with the interview. Will wasn't walking yet, but crawling sure got him everywhere he wanted to go. And into everything he wanted to get into, Brian had already discovered. Gail had told him not to worry. The house was "baby proof," whatever that meant.

As for Will's prospective nanny, Brian didn't know what he'd expected but it hadn't been this mousy little blonde whose big brown eyes looked at him as if he were a hunter and she a rabbit.

She placed Will in the playpen then turned to Brian. "Mr. Kincaid? Is there anything else you'd like to know? I can get you a reference from my last job. My other references are on the resume I brought with me."

He remembered the paper in his hand, the list of questions his sister and sisters-in-law had helped him come up with. He glanced at it again, then tossed it down. "I don't need references. You've got a great one from my brother and his wife. Jay and Gail think you'll be perfect for the job."

"But you're not so sure," she said shrewdly.

So, she was perceptive. He smiled. "No, I think you'll be fine. It's me I'm not sure about."

"I don't understand."

"Look, Faith, if this is going to work, I think we need to be up-front with each other."

She seemed startled but then nodded. "Is it a problem for you that I have a baby, too? I really do believe I can handle both of them. I wouldn't have applied for the job if I didn't. Will won't be neglected, Mr. Kincaid, I can promise you that."

"If I'd thought you'd neglect him you'd be gone by now. First thing is, call me Brian. It's going to get on my nerves to have you calling me Mr. Kincaid all the time." He took a deep breath and continued. "Until five days ago, I didn't even know I had a son. Then his mother died, her lawyer called me, and bam! I'm an instant daddy. It rocked my world, to put it mildly."

Her brown eyes widened. "She never told you?"

"Nope. Not a word."

"Maybe she didn't think you'd care."

Brian stared at her, a little surprised by the comment. "If so, she was wrong." He wouldn't have ignored his responsibilities. But Adrianna had taken that choice out of his hands.

"I'm sorry, I shouldn't have said that. But you did say you wanted us to be honest with each other. Not all men are anxious to…take responsibility."

There was a story there, Brian sensed. "Whatever her reasons, I wasn't told. Which is why you'll notice I know nothing about babies. I've never been married, never lived with a woman. So it's going to be a big adjustment for me to live with not only you but two babies, as well."

"I can understand that." She put her sleeping daughter down on the couch. "I've never lived with anyone, either. At least, not until I had Lily."

"What about her father?" He gestured to the baby. "Is he going to have a problem with this arrangement?"

Faith grimaced. "Lily's father? He took off the minute he heard I was pregnant. He's definitely not in the picture."

Tough break for her, but it was one less complication for him. Which was good since things were complicated enough already. Another thing that was good: Faith was clearly nothing like the women he dated. A sexy, gorgeous woman living with him, distracting him and making him wish she weren't working for him, wouldn't have been smart. Plain, sweet Faith McClain was just the person to take care of his son.

"So, Faith, do you want the job?" He offered his hand.

Slowly, she put her hand in his and shook it. She had a nice handshake. Firm, not limp like so many women's.

"Yes, I do. I think we can make it work."

"I'm sure we can," he said, lying through his teeth.

Just then, Lily woke up and started crying. Will joined in a moment later. Faith picked up her daughter to soothe her while Brian went to take care of his son.

Yeah, he'd completely lost his mind.

CHAPTER FOUR

THREE WEEKS LATER, Faith, Lily, Brian and Will had all moved into a five-bedroom home two streets over from Jay and Gail's house. In the meantime, Faith had kept Will at her apartment during the day and overnight for a couple of nights when Brian had gone to Dallas to pick up some of his and Will's belongings. He'd rented a U-Haul for the most important things and arranged for the rest to be packed and brought to him several days later.

Will was a sweet baby, Faith discovered quickly. But he wasn't the cheerful child she suspected he'd been before his mother's death. He needed a routine badly. And, unfortunately, he needed his mother. She was glad Brian had managed to rent the house prior to closing so they could start getting settled, for Will's sake if nothing else.

With a lot of help from the Kincaids, they had unpacked the boxes and moved in Brian's furniture, as well as the furniture from Faith's apartment. When the rest of Brian and Will's stuff came from

Dallas, they had either stored or sold what they wouldn't be using. Most of the remaining boxes wound up in the fifth bedroom, which was intended to be Brian's office.

Brian had told her he was going to freelance from home until his computer consulting business was up and running. Once he began needing employees, he'd move into an office building. But he didn't seem in a big hurry to do that. Faith had heard the kind of work he did paid very well and figured the rumor must be true or he wouldn't be able to take so much time off. Besides, everything about him said he had money to spare, from the car he drove, a candy-apple-red classic Corvette, to the designer clothes he wore. Even in blue jeans, he looked like he'd stepped out of a magazine ad.

Faith put the babies down for a nap and then sought out Brian in his office. She found him sifting through one of the boxes. He looked up when she came in and smiled. "Don't tell me you got them both down at the same time."

"So far, so good. This is Lily's regular nap time, but Will fights it. I'm trying to establish a routine. Babies do better when they know what to expect."

"Yeah, the poor kid has had a lot of turmoil in his life lately. Maybe getting settled into the house will help."

"I think it will. Just give him some time." She took in the mess around her. "Anything I can do for you here?"

He shook his head and continued to take things out of the cardboard box. "You have enough to do taking care of the babies."

"I can help you unpack a few boxes. They should sleep for at least an hour. More if I'm lucky. Lily's usually a good napper."

"You should nap, then. I know you were up during the night with Will."

"It wasn't for long. He went right back to sleep. So let me help."

He looked like he was about to argue, then shrugged. "Okay, I can use it. I'm trying to make some headway in this room so when the DSL folks come out tomorrow I can get online. I can't do any work without a connection." He pulled a stuffed animal out of the box and set it aside. "I'm going to put in a wireless network. I can add your computer to it, if you want."

"Thanks, but I haven't had Internet access since before Lily was born, so I'm in no hurry. I just used my computer when I brought work home. I'm not even sure it can still get online," she added with a laugh. "It's a dinosaur. A friend of mine gave it to me when she got a new one and that was several years ago."

"I'll take a look at it for you. I might be able to upgrade it and get you online without much problem."

"You don't need to do that."

"It's not a big deal." He stopped what he was doing and turned to her. "You're not a technophobe, are you?"

Faith laughed. "No, I'm computer literate. But with Lily I haven't had much time for it."

"I can understand that. I tried surfing the Web the first few days I had Will by myself. I researched child care when he was asleep." He shook his head. "Way too much information. I did better with the books Adrianna had."

"That must have been tough for you, not knowing anything about children." She opened up another box and started to sort through it. It was filled with photo albums and what looked like mementos. Flipping open one of the albums she saw baby pictures and realized they must have belonged to Will's mother.

"It was tough on both of us. It's a blur, but I think he screamed and cried almost the whole time he wasn't sleeping. Nothing I did seemed to help."

Maybe that explained why Brian tended to disappear whenever he heard the babies crying.

Brian pulled a framed picture out of the box. "This is Will and his mother. I think it must have been taken shortly before she died. Maybe we should put a couple of photos in his room." He handed it to Faith. "Why don't we start a pile of what's going to Will's room and what I'm going to put in the attic for him to have later. The stuff in these boxes is either his or Adrianna's."

No surprise to Faith, Will's mother was a very pretty, very sexy blonde. Exactly the type of woman Brian was rumored to date. Speculation was rampant in Aransas City about whether the third Kincaid brother really intended to settle down there and raise his son. Even before she took the job Faith had heard talk. Everyone, from people in the grocery store to the nurses at the clinic, had an opinion. In the sense of gossip spreading like wildfire, Aransas City was a textbook small town.

She noticed Brian staring at another photo as if he didn't know what to do with it. "If this is hard for you, I can take care of it. Or at least organize everything into what I know Will might need and things I'm not sure about."

"Hard for me?" He looked puzzled for a minute, then shook his head. "I wouldn't say hard. Adrianna and I didn't know each other that well. It's just…" He hesitated before continuing. "It's weird going through her stuff. The movers packed most of this and I just had them transport it all down here. I figured I could go through the stuff once it got here."

He gestured at the cardboard boxes. "Her whole life is all packed up in a bunch of boxes."

"Not her whole life. There's Will."

"True." He sorted through a couple more things. "I feel like I should be able to tell Will about his mother one day, but how can I? I don't know anything about her. She didn't even have family for him to get to know."

Faith bit her lip. What she'd started to say was definitely not something you'd say to your boss. Not if you wanted to keep your job.

"You can go ahead and say it," he told her with some amusement. "You don't exactly have a poker face."

She turned away, picked up a teddy bear and carefully placed it on Will's pile of stuffed animals and assorted toys. "I wasn't going to say anything. It's none of my business."

"We're living in the same house. You're helping me take care of my kid. You have a right to know who I am. And to say what you think."

"I know who you are." Brian might have faults but he had taken responsibility for his son. He was trying hard and she recognized and appreciated that. It couldn't have been easy for him to learn he was a father, especially with it coming out of the blue as it had. Still it was clear he didn't know what to do with Will. Perhaps he would get better at it with time.

"You don't approve of me, do you? Because I didn't know about the baby."

"I didn't say that."

"But I can see you're thinking it. Adrianna and I didn't have a relationship, Faith. We had a good time and then we went our separate ways. She never tried to get in touch with me. She wasn't any more interested in being serious than I was."

"Being pregnant is serious. Take it from me."

He met her gaze. "That's the problem, isn't it? You think I'm a jerk because I wasn't there when she was pregnant."

"I don't think you're a jerk." Who knew how he would have reacted if Adrianna had told him? Faith knew she should give him the benefit of the doubt.

"I'm sorry Lily's father hurt you."

Damn him for reading her so well. She tried to shrug off his comment. "He was a player from the get-go. I should have recognized that. I was naive not to." And she'd paid the price. But he'd given her Lily and she wouldn't have missed out on having her baby girl for anything. Still, she couldn't deny she disapproved of playboys. How could she not? But neither did she believe that Brian would seduce a woman with false promises as Peter Bruce had done to her. He'd played with her dreams and then dumped her the second she became inconvenient.

She glanced at Brian and found him watching

her. Brian Kincaid wouldn't need false promises, she admitted. Dark hair, dark green eyes. *And don't forget hot.*

He could seduce a woman with just a smile. Especially a woman like her, who always fell for the wrong type of man. Thank goodness Brian had no interest in seducing her. She didn't think she'd be much of a challenge for a man like him.

He cleared his throat and, realizing she'd been staring, she turned away. "There's something I wanted to talk to you about," he said. "Two things, really. I think we need to hire a housekeeper. But I want you to hire her. I had a hard enough time hiring a nanny."

"Don't you want me to clean the house?"

"No, I want you to take care of Will. We can have a housekeeper come in once a week. It will save everyone's sanity."

"Are you sure?" The thought of having someone to do the heavy housework was foreign to Faith.

"I hired you to spend time with Will and see to his needs, not to clean my house. I'm sure."

"All right, I'll check into that right away. What else did you want to talk about?"

"Gail tells me there's a program called Mothers' Day Out at the church. It's twice a week, four hours a day. I think we should enroll the babies in it to give you a break. I called them today and there's room."

"You just said you wanted me to take care of Will and that's why you're hiring a housekeeper." She knew about the program but had never used it since she had needed full-time day care to go back to work.

"You are taking care of him. But even nannies need a little time off. No one should work 24/7. What do you say?"

It didn't seem right, but Will was his child, after all. "Of course, if you want Will to go, that's up to you."

"Babies. Plural. Lily should go, too." When she hesitated, he added, "Don't worry, I'll take care of her bill."

"I couldn't ask you to do that." He was already being far more generous than she would have believed when she took the job. Not just her salary and living expenses but all the fringe benefits, and now he was talking about making the job even easier. She felt guilty, as if she weren't doing enough. "Lily will be fine with me."

"They're expecting two babies. Consider it an investment in your sanity." He smiled. "Come on, Faith, let me take care of this. You're doing all the child care, all the cooking. You need some time off. And we haven't discussed it, but if you want a night or two a week off, let me know. Unless I'm out of town, I'll take care of Will and you can make arrangements for Lily."

"You're going to take care of Will by yourself?"

He hadn't shown much interest in doing that so far. He left all the day-to-day care of Will to Faith. He didn't ignore him exactly, he just didn't seem to know how to relate to him. And now he wanted to take care of him by himself?

"Don't sound so shocked. I did it before I hired you."

She decided not to point out that he'd been staying with his brother and that Gail and her daughters had probably helped him out quite a bit. Still, he'd apparently taken care of Will by himself before he'd brought him to Aransas City.

She was weakening. Having nights off wasn't a big deal since she really had nowhere to go, but she might think of something for her and Lily to do simply to give Brian time alone with his son. She thought he and Will would both benefit from that. But time off during the day sounded heavenly, she had to admit. Four hours, twice a week. She could do the grocery shopping without crying babies. She could even get a haircut without holding Lily on her lap. However, she felt duty bound to protest. "That's very generous. But one of the reasons I took this job was so Lily wouldn't have to be in day care. She was sick constantly when I was working full-time."

"Gail says they're pretty good about insisting sick kids stay home, and if she starts getting colds a lot you can reevaluate. You're not a slave, Faith.

Taking a little time off will be good for both you and the kids."

"You're not going to take no for an answer, are you?"

"What do you think?" His lips curved into a devilish smile.

That wicked smile of his was too damn attractive was what she thought. "All right. Thank you."

"Good, we'll take them in tomorrow and get everything set up."

He was her boss. And even if he hadn't been, he was miles out of her league. Brian Kincaid was entirely too good-looking—and, worse, way too nice—for her peace of mind.

Lily's father had been nice and charming, too, she reminded herself. Right up until the time she'd told him she was pregnant.

CHAPTER FIVE

BRIAN AND FAITH drove separate cars to the church the next morning, Faith taking both children with her so she'd have their car seats when she picked them up.

First Brian was going to see his brother Mark. After that he planned to meet Jay for lunch and then go over to the clinic to talk to the doctors and their staff about their computer needs. Although medical programs weren't his specialty, he'd been reading up on what was available both to help with patient care and in the business and billing aspects of their practice so that he could help Jay and his partners decide what programs and system would best suit them.

He parked his car beside Faith's then went to help her get the kids out. "How are you going to do this when I'm not here? You can't carry both of them and all their stuff." He still wasn't sure why, but every time you set foot out of the house with a young child, you had to haul around a suitcase full of crap with you. Double the kids and you doubled the amount of crap.

She settled Lily on her hip and swung the diaper bag onto her shoulder. "I've been thinking about that and I think we should buy a twin stroller. It will be a lot easier for me to take both babies with me that way. I'd be able to take them on walks, too. I'll pay for half of it, since it's for Lily, as well as Will."

"You're not paying for half of it. That's ridiculous." But he wasn't surprised she'd offered. Or that she was set to argue about it. "Make this one easy on me. Please," he said before she could get started. "Just charge it to me, okay?"

She nodded, but not without sulking. Her lips were full and looked surprisingly sexy set in a pout. *She's the nanny,* he reminded himself. Not someone he should flirt with.

Will was crying but, to Brian's surprise, the baby quieted when he took him out of the car seat. Usually Brian only made him cry harder. Imitating Faith, he settled the little guy on his hip. His son stared at him with solemn eyes as he carried his son into the church, following Faith and Lily. "Don't worry, you'll like it," he told him, wondering if that were true.

"Bah," Will said.

They enrolled both kids and Brian paid for them. Then he went to make sure that Will was settled and being well looked after. The kid was laughing with delight as one of the caregivers played peekaboo with him, both of them oblivious to the chaos surrounding them. Faith, however, seemed to have a million questions still, so Brian left her to it.

The sooner he got out of there, the better. All those young kids in one place made him break out in a cold sweat. Older kids weren't so bad, but Brian hadn't been around much since his brothers had married and their wives had started popping out small fry. He wasn't sure what he'd do at Thanksgiving when he'd have to sit down to dinner with not only his son, but all the extended families and their kids. *Zoo* would be a kind description of that scene.

He'd realized on the way to the church that he needed to buy another car. He couldn't expect Faith to use her car for all the errands. He could pay for her gas, but there was a matter of wear and tear, and her car had obviously already seen a lot of miles. And she sure couldn't use his 'Vette to take the babies around in.

He glanced at the seat beside him and winced. Will had spit up on it on the way down to Aransas City, and while Brian had cleaned it up as soon as he could, he'd apparently missed some spots. His car wasn't any more built for kids than he was. It was a classic, lovingly cared for. Rather than give it up, he'd stored it while he was out of the country. And now it had spit-up on it. And that wasn't the worst of it.

In order to get the playpen and the other things he'd deemed essential in, he'd had to cram everything he could in the trunk, then tie it down. He had consciously avoided looking at what he suspected was a scratch on the car's otherwise pristine paint job.

But what kind of car did you buy to haul kids and their stuff around in? No way was he getting a minivan. The thought made him slightly nauseous. He had to draw the line somewhere.

A few minutes later, he pulled up in front of Mark's house. He knew his brother would be there since he'd talked to him that morning. Cat had recently had their third child, a boy they named Cullen. Mark periodically took time off to help her with the kids.

"Hey, how's it going?" Mark asked, letting him in.

"That's what I came to ask you."

"It's not too bad today, but Max is at school and Miranda is at Mothers' Day Out. Once they get home, it will be chaos as usual."

"I didn't see Miranda when I took Will in. How are Cat and the baby?"

"They're great. Cullen actually sleeps, unlike Max at that age." As if on cue, a baby's cry came from the other room. "Well, sometimes he sleeps," he said with a grin. "Why don't you come with me? Cat's out with Gail so I'm on duty. She and her sister have some new scheme cooking for Thanksgiving."

Brian followed him into the baby's room and watched Mark lift Cullen out of his crib and change him. Mark looked calm, competent…and most of all, happy. Brian wondered if he'd ever feel like that. Like a real father instead of an imposter.

"I'm going to warm up his bottle. Want to feed him?"

"Are you kidding? He's too little." Brian still had a hard time with Will; he couldn't imagine feeding a tiny baby like the one Mark was holding.

"Come on, don't be a chicken. I'll show you. It's not much different from feeding Will."

"Oh, yes, it is. Will's big enough to hold his own bottle. Besides, I might hurt him or something."

"Only if you drop him." Mark laughed and took the baby with him to the kitchen.

He warmed up the milk and tested it. Thank God Kara Long had at least explained bottles to him before handing Will over to him, Brian thought. He sure as hell wouldn't have known anything about warming them. "How do you know what to do with him? Doesn't it make you nervous when Cat leaves you with him?"

"This is our third, remember? You stop being nervous after the first. But I'll admit, the first time Cat left me alone with Max, I thought I was having a heart attack every time he cried. It got easier, though."

They went to the den and Mark sat in the rocking

chair with the baby to give him his bottle. Brian watched them for a moment before he brought up what had been on his mind since he'd found out Will really was his son. He didn't try to finesse it, he just blurted it out. "I don't know if I can do this. I don't know if I can be a father."

Mark sent him a sharp glance. "You already are a father. And you told Jay you wouldn't give him up, so I don't see you have much choice but to figure it out."

Brian stood and started pacing. "I don't want to give him up. But maybe he'd be better off with someone who…knows what they're doing."

"That's why you hired a nanny. Why are you getting cold feet at this point? Isn't the nanny working out?"

"Faith is great. That's not the problem. The problem is me. I walk in and see all this baby stuff and I still can't believe it's in my house. Belongs to my son. I hear him crying and think, 'Whose kid is that? I wish they'd make him quit,' and then I remember I'm the one who's supposed to be comforting him. I'm responsible for him. A baby."

"It's a big adjustment."

"Everyone says I'll get used to it, but it's been weeks and I haven't so far. What if I never do?"

"You haven't been living with him very long. Give it time. Give each other time."

Brian just shook his head. He wasn't sure time would help. Or that anything would. "I don't think he likes me. He cries almost every time I touch him."

"He's had it rough lately. It'll get better. Don't take it personally."

"It's kind of hard not to." He squeezed the bridge of his nose. Don't take it personally that his own son liked the nanny—hell, liked everyone— better than him.

"Is something else wrong?"

He sat and propped his arms on his knees, staring at the floor unseeingly. "Fathers—good fathers—are supposed to love their children. I don't know what I feel. Other than totally, hopelessly confused." Desperate for an answer, he looked at his oldest brother.

Mark put the baby up to his shoulder and patted his back. "What's this about, Brian? Are you saying you want to give Will up?"

"No." Will was his son, his responsibility. "I'm saying this fatherhood thing…I suck at it. I'm afraid I'll be…like him. Like our father." There. He'd finally admitted what he feared most.

Mark frowned. "That's bullshit. He was an abusive bastard. You could never be anything like him."

"I don't have to be abusive to be a lousy father like he was."

"Look, Brian, you may not be father-of-the-year

material, but you're trying. Don't compare yourself to that worthless bastard."

"I hardly remember him. All I remember was him telling me to leave him the hell alone. One time, I think I was about five, he locked me in a closet because I was bugging him. Miranda—Ava—let me out, but she didn't find me until I'd been in there for hours. I spent the rest of the time until he left trying to stay out of his way. I was so damn happy when I realized he wasn't coming back and I didn't have to be afraid he'd walk through the door and yell at me. Or worse."

"He played mind games with all of us. Don't let him ruin what you could have with your son."

"Will doesn't even know me. He wants his mother, not me. But the poor kid's stuck with me."

"Do you want my advice?"

Brian shot him a dirty look. "Why the hell else would I be here telling you all this crap? Believe me, admitting I'm a big fat failure at fatherhood is not my idea of fun."

Mark smiled. "You're not a failure. Take care of him. Don't let Faith do it all. You need to feed him, bathe him, read to him. Comfort him when he cries. Just be with him. Before long you'll look at Will and you won't be able to imagine what your life was like without him."

"You make it sound so easy." It couldn't be that simple, could it?

"Being a parent is a challenge. But loving your kids," he looked at his own son and smiled, "there's nothing easier."

FAITH WAS FEEDING the babies when Brian walked into the kitchen that evening. She was wearing a good bit of what she'd tried to get Will to eat. Luckily, Lily wasn't nearly as messy with her finger food. Yet. Give her a few months, though, and the kitchen would probably look like a war zone at mealtime.

"Hi. How was your day?" she asked.

"Not bad. I think we've decided on what they want at the clinic so I'll start work there over the Thanksgiving holiday. They want it installed and all the bugs worked out by the new year."

"That's good. You've seemed a little…antsy. I wondered if it was because you wanted to get back to work." She left Will to his banana and picked up the baby-food jar and spoon to feed Lily. It wasn't easy feeding two babies at once, but she was getting the hang of it.

"Yeah, I guess I have. I'm not used to having so much time off. But I'm looking forward to running my own business rather than working for someone else."

"Will you be traveling overseas, like you did before? It must be exciting living in other countries." Faith had rarely been out of Texas. She'd always had a secret desire to travel, but now that she had Lily, she knew she wouldn't be traveling for a long time.

"No, I think I'll have enough to do right here. Besides, it will be better for Will if I'm not out of the country for long periods of time."

"Will you miss it?"

He looked thoughtful. "Haven't so far. I really enjoyed London, and China was interesting, but I was ready to come home. I'm glad I was able to experience different cultures, but I like the U.S., too. I haven't spent a lot of time in one place, though, since I got my master's."

She watched Will take a bite of banana and smear it into the tray. "It's a huge change for you to live in Aransas City after all the other places you've been, isn't it?"

He laughed. "Yeah, you could say that. London it isn't. But most of my family is here so it seemed reasonable to move down here instead of settling in Dallas. And there's no way I would have tried to take Will overseas without any of them near." He picked up an apple from the bowl on the counter. "Speaking of family, what are your plans for Thanksgiving? Are you going to see your family?" He took a bite of apple.

She opened a jar of peas to give to Lily. Will wouldn't touch peas but Lily loved them. "I just thought Lily and I would have a quiet day here. My parents died several years ago, so I don't have anyone to visit."

"Spend it with my family, then."

"That wasn't a ploy for sympathy and I wasn't fishing for an invitation. Thanks, but we'd better not."

"Why not? There's going to be a ton of people there. Two more won't matter. Dinner is at Ava and Jack's house. It's the only one big enough to hold everyone. Although, I'm not convinced it will. Of course, nobody listens to me."

It sounded like fun. She should turn him down but she found that she really didn't want to. "If you're sure, okay, we'd love to come."

"Good, that's settled." He leaned against the counter and continued munching on the apple for a moment. "I meant to ask, how was the first day of Mothers' Day Out?"

She smiled. "An unqualified success. Both Will and Lily had a wonderful time. The people were great. It seems like a good program."

"I figured it would be since Gail vouched for it. She said both she and her sister—Mark's wife, Cat—have taken their kids there. In fact, Mark said his daughter Miranda was there today, although I didn't see her."

He took another bite of apple and chewed. "So what did you do today on your first day of freedom?"

"Oh, this and that. I hired a housekeeper." No way could she tell him what else she'd done. It would sound pathetic, and that was the last way she wanted to appear to Brian.

"That's good." He didn't say anything else but she felt him staring at her. Heat rose in her face. Surely she didn't look that different, did she?

"What happened to your glasses?"

"I got contacts." That was the first thing she'd done. She'd been wanting them for some time but couldn't justify spending the money until now. "Why, do I look funny? I feel a little odd without my glasses."

"No. Your eyes look bigger." He tilted his head. "You did something to your hair, too."

She gave Will a bowl of Cheerios and turned to Lily to feed her another bite of peas. "I had it cut. I wanted something easier to manage." And she'd used a rinse she'd bought at the grocery store to lighten it, but she wasn't going to tell him that. "I thought men weren't supposed to notice things like that. Unless they're gay."

Brian grinned. "Nope. Purely heterosexual."

No joke.

"Your hair is blonder, too. It looks more like your daughter's now."

She gave him a dirty look. "Fine, I had a make-over. Sort of. I was tired of looking frumpy. I wanted a change."

"You didn't look frumpy."

She shot him a disbelieving look. "Right."

"Do you have a date? Is that what this is about?"

"Of course I don't have a date." When had she had time to find someone to date? "I just wanted a change. Can we talk about something else now?"

She picked up Will's food and then wiped his face, though it didn't do a lot of good. "That's right, sweetheart. We'll go have a bath in just a minute."

"I'll do it. And then I'll put him to bed."

Faith stared at him. What had gotten into him? He'd never volunteered for bedtime duty before. "Brian, that's part of my job."

"Doesn't mean you have to do it every night. If you're worried I don't know how, I did it before you came to work for me."

He had that stubborn look, so she knew his mind was made up. "I realize that. That's not what I was worried about."

He raised an eyebrow. "We've already discussed your nonpoker face."

She laughed. "All right. If you're sure, I'll finish up with Lily and put her to bed, then I'll see what I can come up with for dinner."

"Sounds like a deal."

"Call me if you need me," she said.

He lifted Will out of his high chair. "We'll be fine. But thanks."

Maybe she should date, she thought as she took

Lily to her room. That might keep her mind off her very appealing boss. Unfortunately, single men were hard to come by in Aransas City. And those she'd met just didn't interest her.

Except the one who was off-limits.

CHAPTER SIX

"WHAT'S WITH ALL the food?" Brian asked when he came home the next day after having been in Corpus Christi with a prospective client. "I came in through the kitchen and it looks like you had a cooking marathon. Or raided a bakery."

Faith was seated cross-legged on the floor in the den with both babies. Will sat in her lap tugging on her hair as she tried to play patty-cake with him; Lily lay on a pallet on her stomach playing with one of those interactive toys that made all sorts of sounds. He'd almost grown used to the noise level of the kids being awake.

Faith looked up at him, laughing, and it struck him as it had the day before how pretty she was. In a whole-some sort of way. But on Faith wholesome looked good. Damn good. Brian wasn't sure he approved of this new Faith. He needed plain, not pretty.

"There's more in the refrigerator. We need to decide what you want to eat right away and what to freeze. But I didn't cook any of it." She straightened her mouth but her dimples still peeked out. "The casserole ladies have discovered you."

Yeah, way too pretty. "What's a casserole lady?"

"You know, whenever a man is widowed or a new single man comes to town, they bake for him. A friend of mine calls them casserole ladies."

"All that stuff is from women?" The countertop was covered with food. Cakes, cookies, pies. He'd thought Faith had lost it.

"Every blessed thing. It was Mothers' Day Out that did it. Now they all know you're single and have an absolutely adorable son." She laughed again when Will made a raspberry sound. "That's right, sweetheart." She ruffled his hair. "You are one adorable baby."

"I don't get it. Most of those women are married." Brian sat beside her, then stretched out on his side and propped himself up on his elbow to get comfortable.

Faith put Will down and he promptly crawled over to the toy Lily had been playing with and started banging it on the floor. Faith propped Lily up against a pillow and gave her a toy, which she threw down immediately.

"Most of the women who use the Mothers' Day Out program are married, but not all of them. And the ones who are married have single sisters, cousins and friends. So you'd better brace yourself."

She paused and added, "But you probably don't mind, do you?"

He shrugged and said, "Depends on what they look like. Were any of them hot?"

He looked at her from beneath his lashes as he handed Lily the toy she'd tossed away.

Faith's jaw literally dropped. "Brian! I can't believe you said that. That's so shallow."

He laughed. "You should have seen your face."

"Men are so predictable."

"It's one of our charms."

Lily flung the toy he'd just given her, squealing as she did so. He picked it up and handed it back to her.

"Now you've done it," Faith warned. "She'll have you doing that a thousand times. She never tires of that game."

She threw it away once again and had him smiling. She was a beautiful baby, very fair, with big, blue eyes. "Wonder why she didn't get your brown eyes?" he said aloud.

"She has her father's eyes."

Lily toppled over and started to cry. He helped her sit up again and was rewarded with a grin. It depressed him sometimes that Lily seemed to like him more than Will did. "Is that a good thing or a bad thing?"

"Oh, it's a good thing. He's attractive, even if he is a jerk."

"Do you miss him?"

She'd been watching Will make faces at himself in the mirror but at that, she looked at Brian. "No. At first I did, but it didn't take me long to realize that a man who would desert his pregnant girlfriend and unborn child like he did wasn't worth it."

"True." But somehow he didn't think she'd gotten over the guy as easily as she'd like him to believe. "Have you had a date since Lily was born?"

Faith laughed. "I'm a single mother. Who has time to date?"

Brian didn't answer, just raised an eyebrow.

"I'm not hung up on him, if that's what you're thinking."

"I didn't say you were." Even if he did suspect that to be the case.

"You don't believe me, do you?"

Brian shrugged. "It's none of my business. I didn't mean for you to get bent out of shape. It was just a question."

"I'm not bent out of shape. But now you answer a question for me. Have you had a date since you took custody of Will?" She picked up Lily and cuddled her.

"No." Will crawled over to him and sat, looking at him solemnly before he started chanting syllables. Sometimes he strung them together, but he didn't make a lot of sense yet. He'd been saying

"Mama," though, since the day Brian had picked him up from Kara Long.

"Why not?"

"I just haven't had time for women." Which wasn't quite true. He could have made time if he'd wanted. Maybe he should now that his life had settled down a bit.

Faith looked at him as if to say she'd made her point, then got up with Lily in her arms. "It's time for the babies' dinner. Why don't you bring Will into the kitchen and we'll feed them."

He let the change of subject pass and followed her with Will on his hip.

Faith put Lily in her high chair and Brian did the same with Will. He was actually starting to feel more comfortable doing the daily stuff that having a baby involved. It still astounded him that he had a son, but not nearly as much as it had at first.

Faith went to the refrigerator and started pulling out baby food. "Since Lily was born I've been struggling to support us, so I haven't had a lot of time for men. And, frankly, they hardly seem worth the trouble after my last experience. I'm not hung up on Lily's father. I just have no use for men right now."

"Not all men are like him." What a waste that she thought men were too much trouble.

Faith snorted. "Right. It doesn't matter anyway.

Even if someone asked me out, who would stay with Lily?"

He ought to be glad she hadn't started dating. He didn't want her to fall for some guy, get serious about him and quit her job, did he? On the other hand, if Faith was dating someone—anyone—then maybe he'd quit wondering about what it would be like to kiss her. Because the past two days he'd found himself fantasizing about that far more often than he should.

It would be a monumental mistake. If flirting with the nanny was a no-no, then kissing her was definitely out. *He* was the one who needed a date.

"You could ask Roxy," he said, referring to one of Jay and Gail's daughters. "She's almost thirteen, and if I was here with Will, I'm sure they'd let her take care of Lily. She helps out with Jason all the time, so I know she's good with babies. Both their girls are."

"You're very annoying sometimes." Faith handed him a bowl of finger food to give to Will, then sat down to feed Lily.

"You're just annoyed because I have a point."

"Fine, if someone asks me out, I'll think about it. Satisfied?"

Not really. He was afraid nothing was really going to satisfy him until he kissed Faith. And that was so not going to happen.

FAITH KNEW she shouldn't have been surprised when two days after their conversation about dating and moving on, Brian called her and said not to bother fixing dinner for him because he had a date. She certainly had no business wondering who he was with and how that date was going. She'd practically thrown him into the waiting casserole ladies' arms, after all.

Besides that, he was so obviously not interested in Faith. Why else would he have pushed her to start dating again? He felt sorry for her. Probably thought she couldn't get a date. Well, she wasn't going to sit around like a pathetic lump mooning over her boss. She picked up the phone and called Gail. Since Faith had begun working for Brian, she and Gail had become good friends.

They chatted a bit and then Faith came straight to the point. "Did you mean it about fixing me up with a friend of yours?"

"Of course. But what changed your mind? Last time I mentioned it, you were totally against going on a blind date."

"I just wasn't ready then. I am now. But I need to ask a favor. I'll make sure Brian can take care of Will whatever night it is, but do you think Roxy could watch Lily for me? Brian mentioned she helps you and I thought—"

Gail interrupted. "That's a great idea. Roxy loves babies and she's wonderful with Jason. I won't let her babysit alone yet, but with Brian there, she'll be fine. I'm so glad you changed your mind."

Faith wasn't sure she was, but she'd taken that first step so she might as well go through with it.

"He's a great guy, Faith," Gail continued enthusiastically. "I know you two will get along. His name is Allen Carver. He's a doctor, someone Jay knows, actually, who lives in Corpus Christi. I'll give him your number as soon as we get off the phone."

"Thanks." They talked a little more, then hung up. The phone rang a few minutes later and, sure enough, it was her blind date. Gail must have called him immediately, she decided, then wondered what exactly her friend had said about her to have the guy contacting her so quickly. She agreed to go to dinner the next evening, though she warned him she might have to reschedule if it didn't fit in with her boss's plans.

Faith took out her contacts and put on her sweats. After checking on the children, who were both sleeping soundly, she settled down in the den to watch a romantic comedy on TV and pretend she wasn't waiting up for Brian.

AS BRIAN LET HIMSELF IN the back door, he realized he couldn't remember the last time he'd gotten home from a date by ten o'clock. At least he'd been the one to cut out early. Corinna had been perfectly willing to make a night of it. At her apartment, yet.

She'd reminded him how much fun they'd had the last time he'd seen her. But tonight she just hadn't interested him. She was gorgeous, he'd grant her that. But he didn't believe she had two thoughts in her head. Worse, she agreed with everything he said and seemed to have no opinions of her own. Boring with a capital *B*.

Since when do you care about a woman's brains? he asked himself. Especially a woman who was built like Corinna.

He'd changed, he realized. He wanted something more than what he'd been content with in the past. But there were plenty of women to date, after all. Next time he'd be a little more discerning. Someone not only beautiful, but someone who could carry on a decent conversation, as well.

As he walked down the hallway going to his bedroom, he noticed the lights and TV were on in the den. Faith was on the couch, fast asleep.

He stopped for a minute and looked at her. Her glasses had slipped down her nose and her head rested on her arm. As he stood watching, her lips curved into a surprisingly wicked grin. He wished he knew what she was dreaming about.

If he left her there, she'd be cramped and cold by morning. Assuming one of the babies didn't wake up before then, crying for her. He went to check on the kids and found them both sleeping soundly. He went back to the den and leaned down, touching Faith's shoulder to wake her.

Her eyes blinked open and she smiled. A warm, welcoming smile. "Hi," she said huskily.

"Hi." He returned the smile as she snuggled back into the couch and closed her eyes again, obviously still half-asleep. "Don't you want to go to bed?"

"Hmm."

He was tempted, very tempted, to run his hand down her arm. He controlled the impulse and spoke more loudly. "Faith, wake up. It's time to go to bed."

"Huh?" Her eyes opened, widened. She sat up suddenly, catching him off guard and smashing her head into his nose.

Brian swore, holding his nose as Faith looked around wildly. "What time is it? What's going on? Are the babies all right?"

He sat down beside her, his hand still covering his throbbing nose. "Calm down, will you? The babies are fine. But I'm not. I think my nose is broken."

She took off her glasses and rubbed her eyes before putting them back on. "I'm sorry. You startled me."

"Yeah, I got that."

She pushed his hand aside. "Let me see." She pressed gently on the bridge. "It's not bleeding."

"I'll live." Her lips were full. Close and inviting. Her brown eyes were dark, filled with concern. He started to reach out and run his thumb over those plump, pretty lips until he remembered he had no business running his thumb over anything of Faith's. Especially not that luscious mouth.

She averted her gaze and shifted away from him. "I can't believe I fell asleep on the couch. I don't think I lasted ten minutes into the movie. What time is it?"

"About ten-thirty."

"You're home early. Wasn't your date fun?"

"It was okay. She had to be at work early tomorrow so we called it a night," he lied. He got up. "I'm beat, I'm going to hit the sack."

"Me, too. Good night." She walked to the hallway that led to the bedrooms while Brian stayed in the den. At the doorway, she stopped and looked back at him. "Oh, I forgot. I have a favor to ask you."

"Sure, what is it?"

"Can you take care of Will tomorrow night? I have a dinner date."

A dinner date? She had a date? What happened to not having time for men? Men being too much trouble? She must have actually listened to him when he'd spouted all that crap the other night.

"Not a problem. Good night," he told her, thankful she was gone before he said—or did—something he'd regret.

CHAPTER SEVEN

"I THINK LILY WANTS her mommy, but she settled down after I gave her the binky and rubbed her back," Roxy said after checking on the baby. They'd heard Lily fussing and Roxy had insisted that it was her job to go to her.

"What's a binky?"

"The pacifier. That's what we call it, anyway. Jason calls it his baby. Nobody knows why."

Brian looked out the window again but there was no sign of Faith. Will, thankfully, was down for the count. Roxy had tired him out playing with him. It amazed Brian that a twelve-year-old girl was so capable around the babies. Brian wouldn't have known to give Lily a pacifier, for instance. Will didn't have one. Or did he?

"Will doesn't have a pacifier. Is he supposed to?"

"Some babies do and some don't. You'd have found it with his stuff if he used one."

That's true, he realized. Surely Kara Long would have given him one if Will had needed it. He felt somewhat reassured that he hadn't traumatized the poor kid by losing his pacifier.

"Are you waiting up for Faith, Uncle Brian?"

He turned away from the window and glanced at her. "No, why do you ask?"

"You've been looking out the window every ten minutes. That's what Jay does when Mom's gone and Jason's being a pain. But Will's asleep. You don't have to worry."

"I thought she was going to be back early, is all. It's the first time she's left Lily at night." At least, he believed it was since she'd said she hadn't dated. He figured she'd have been more concerned about leaving her daughter with a babysitter for the first time.

"It's only nine-thirty and she's called twice."

"Once."

"Nuh-uh. She called to check on Lily again while you were putting Will to bed." A knowing look came over her face, strangely mature for her years. "You didn't want Faith to go out, did you, Uncle Brian?"

Busted by a twelve-year-old. "It doesn't bother me at all if she goes out," he lied. "I just thought she'd be more worried about Lily."

Roxy didn't comment but Brian could've sworn he heard her giggle. She started picking up toys and putting them away. "Mom says people like babysitters who clean up. Do you think Faith will ask me to sit for her again?"

"I'm sure she will." Unable to help himself, he gazed out the window again but there was still no sign of a car. He had a good view of the front porch. He wondered if Roxy would rat him out if he watched Faith and her date say good-night. He shot her a glance. Oh, yeah, she would tell Faith in a nanosecond.

"I get to start babysitting by myself soon. I can take care of Will sometimes, too, if you want me to. When Faith isn't here, I mean."

"Thanks, Rox. You're really good with babies. Will and Lily sure like you."

She beamed at the praise. "Thanks. I've helped Mom with Jason since he was born. Mel has, too, but I'm the oldest so I'm the most help."

Brian hid a smile. Having finished tidying up the toys, Roxy sat on the couch and tucked her legs under her, prepared to chat. "Are Faith and Lily coming to Aunt Ava's for Thanksgiving? Mom said she told you to ask them."

He stopped himself from glancing out the window again. "Faith said they would. She doesn't have any family to spend the holidays with."

"She and Lily can share our family. We have a big one."

"We sure do."

Roxy looked at him a little anxiously. "Cole's not really my cousin, though. I mean, he's not a blood relative. So we're not like, related or anything. Not really."

Cole Williams was Ava's sixteen-year-old stepson. "Technically Cole's not your family. Why?"

Roxy turned away but not before he saw her color rise. "Oh, I get it. So, you've got a thing for Cole, huh?"

She nodded miserably. "He doesn't even know I'm alive," she said dramatically.

Poor Rox, he almost certainly didn't. If Cole was anything like Brian was at sixteen, he would have other things on his mind besides a pseudocousin four years younger than him. "Wait until you're a little older. Then he'll notice."

"I'm almost thirteen. I'm not a baby."

"No, of course you're not," he said soothingly, though to him twelve pretty much sounded like a baby. He didn't remember much about being her age. But he remembered the year before. When he was eleven, he'd been busy trying to understand why his mother had abandoned him and praying Mark wouldn't get sick of him and Jay and send them to social services.

Not that Mark had ever given him reason to believe he'd do that, but Brian had worried regardless. But instead of being good, he'd been an incredible pain in Mark's ass. He wasn't sure why he'd been that way unless it was because he wanted Mark to prove he'd love him no matter what he did.

"Cole thinks I'm a baby, though," Roxy continued glumly. "Last time I saw him, he patted me on the head, *exactly* like he does Mel."

"Cheer up, Roxy. He's far from ready to settle down and by the time he is you'll be all grown-up and you probably won't give him the time of day."

"But I don't want to wait forever. I mean, you're *old* and you haven't settled down yet."

Ouch. But to an almost-thirteen-year-old, thirty-two was undoubtedly ancient. "I just haven't found the right woman." He wasn't about to tell her he didn't believe there was a right woman for him.

"Mom says she wonders if you'll ever settle down. She says you're good with Will and that you're trying real hard with him, though. She said it kinda surprised her at first since you're such a stud with the women and all."

At a loss for words, Brian stared at her. "Your mother told you that?"

Guilt washed over her face. "Well, she didn't exactly tell *me*…. She and Aunt Cat were talking and they didn't know I could hear them."

It didn't surprise him to know his sisters-in-law had been discussing him. They were women, after all. Brian curbed an impulse to ask what else they'd said. He wasn't sure he wanted to know. "I think I hear a car," he said, thankful for the distraction. "I bet that's Faith."

A few minutes later, she walked in. He'd been with Will before she left so he hadn't seen her go out. She wore a light pink sweater that hugged her curves and a short black skirt that showed off long, shapely legs. Her hair was down, feathered around her face and she'd done something to her eyes to make them appear even darker and larger. She looked pretty and, more than that, hot, which annoyed the hell out of him for reasons he didn't care to analyze.

Roxy had bounded up the minute she'd heard Faith. "Lily was fussy earlier, but she's fine now," she began telling her as they walked toward the hall.

"I'm sure she is. Why don't we go check on her again, though? Just to be sure."

"I'll take Roxy home when she's ready," Brian said. He was tempted to ask Faith about her date, but restrained himself. How lame was that? It was none of his business how her date had gone.

She looked at him for the first time since she'd come in, and smiled. "Thanks, but you don't need to do that. I'll do it if you'll stay with the kids."

"It's not a problem."

"Well, if you're sure. Let me pay her first. Thanks."

"So did you have fun?" he heard Roxy ask as

they left the room. But despite straining his ears to hear, he didn't catch Faith's answer.

THERE HAS TO BE SOMETHING good to eat in here, Faith thought as she rummaged through the refrigerator. What happened to the grapes? She'd just bought them the day before. Surely Brian and Roxy hadn't eaten all of them. After an exhaustive search, she found them, lodged behind an extralarge jar of applesauce.

"What are you doing?" Brian said.

She jumped and turned around, hugging the bowl of grapes to her breast. "You scared me to death." How long had he been standing there, staring at her butt? She tugged at her skirt, took the grapes to the table and sat down.

"What does it look like? I'm eating." She knew she sounded cranky but hunger did that to her.

He took a seat, too, and plucked some grapes from the bowl. "I thought you had a dinner date."

"I did. I'm...still hungry." She moved the bowl closer to her. He'd had all evening to eat them. They were hers now.

"Didn't you like the restaurant?"

"It was fine. I just didn't eat a lot."

"Why?" He popped a grape into his mouth while he waited for her answer.

Tapping her fingers on the table, she frowned at

him. "Because I was nervous, okay? I can't eat very much when I'm nervous."

"Why were you nervous?"

How dense could a man be? "Because it was my first date since I had Lily." Actually, her first date since long before that. Her first date since Lily's no-good father had hightailed it out of town.

He reached for another grape, grinning when she snatched the bowl out of his way. "Where did you go to dinner?"

"Pinero's. It's in Corpus Christi. Do you know it?" Italian. Her favorite. Too bad she had barely touched her entreé.

"Yeah, I know it. It's where a guy takes a woman he really wants to impress." He got up and opened the pantry, returning to the table with a box of gingersnaps.

Her mouth watered. "Could I have some of those?"

He smiled and offered her the box. "Unlike you, I'll share." They munched in silence a moment and then he said, "So, did he impress you?"

"I wouldn't say impress, exactly. He was nice," she said cautiously. Very nice. Maybe even a little too nice. But then, these days she had a suspicious mind where men were concerned. Allen had been a perfect gentleman, though. He'd kissed her good-night, but he hadn't been pushy or offensive about it. It wasn't his fault the kiss had done nothing for her.

"Did you go anywhere else?"

Why was he so curious? "No, there wasn't time. But Allen mentioned the Ellington. It's a jazz club, I think." .

Brian laughed but didn't say anything.

"What?" She picked up another cookie. "Why is that funny? Isn't it a good place to go?"

"Oh, yeah, it's good." His amused gaze met hers. "Very good. Very classy. Very expensive."

"And? There's obviously something you're not telling me."

He ate another gingersnap before answering. "Soft lights, sexy music, fancy wine list. Atmosphere in spades. It's the kind of place you take a woman you want to talk into bed."

She stared at him. "Oh, come on. He wouldn't think I'd sleep with him just because he took me to an expensive club."

Brian waved his finger in the air. "Let's not forget the first part of the date. The classy, pricey, *romantic* restaurant. Yeah, I'd say it's a move."

"Maybe he just wanted to show me a nice time? Without an ulterior motive."

He didn't look convinced. "All right," he conceded. "It's possible."

"But not likely."

Brian shrugged. "He's a guy and you're a beautiful woman. He might not think it's a given, but I'll bet he thinks wining and dining you might get him closer to getting lucky." He paused and added, "Why, are you going to the Ellington next time?"

The little thrill she'd felt when he'd said she was beautiful faded. She gave him a dirty look. "I don't see that it's any of your business." Scratch that second date. *Men.* "And there's not going to be a next time."

"Did you decide that before or after I clued you in?"

His eyes were laughing and she wanted to pinch him. "Before," she lied. She'd been willing to give Allen another chance. But now she'd be so suspicious of his every move it wouldn't be worth it. She rose to put the grapes back in the refrigerator.

"I suppose you know all this because that's how you operate." She closed the door and leaned against it. "Tell me, Brian, where did you take the casserole lady the other night?" she challenged.

"She wasn't a casserole lady. She was a flight attendant I met a few months ago. I ran into her again when I was in Corpus Christi the other day."

"Okay, but you didn't answer my question. Is that how you operate?"

None of your business, her mind chanted. But he'd annoyed her and she couldn't let it go.

He got up and walked over to her. He didn't speak but reached out to touch her hair, letting the ends trail over his fingers. "Why do you want to know, Faith?"

Tension filled the air. She should know better than to play with fire and Brian Kincaid was an explosion just waiting to detonate.

"I don't." She moved away, hoping it didn't look like the full scale retreat it was. "It's late, I'm going to bed."

"Faith."

She halted at the door and looked back at him. He smiled, a sexy smile that made her wish she was more like one of those sophisticated, gorgeous women he dated rather than plain-as-apple-pie Faith McClain.

"For what it's worth, I like to think I'm smoother than that."

"We all need our illusions, don't we?" She smiled sweetly and left, his laughter trailing behind her. He was smooth, all right. And he damn well knew it, no matter what she said.

CHAPTER EIGHT

DURING THE WEEK leading up to Thanksgiving, Brian kept busy with a new client, putting in a new system for a small firm in Corpus Christi. The actual work was enjoyable, but the paperwork it generated wasn't. He might have to hire an assistant before long to keep up with it. Still, for now it was a good thing because it gave him less time to think about Faith. She hadn't gone on another date since the one with Dr. Smooth, which pleased him more than he wanted to admit.

He hadn't gone on another date, either. He rationalized it, telling himself he hadn't had time and it was easier to come home and play with the babies and eat dinner with Faith than to go through the trouble of a date. Besides, Will needed his father to be at home with him in the evenings.

Mark hadn't been the only one who'd told him he needed to spend time with his son. Gail and Cat had given him a bundle of books on child development and child care, and every damn one of them stressed how important it was for a father to be involved in his child's upbringing. And since the last thing Brian wanted was to be anything like his own father, he tried his best to do the right thing for the kid.

Thanksgiving morning he went to get Will dressed for the day at Ava's house. He put him in a pair of denim overalls that snapped at the crotch and a long-sleeve shirt. The kid had outgrown nearly everything his mother had bought him but these overalls had been a larger size. Brian wondered if he could get Faith to pick up some more clothes for Will. That was part of a nanny's job, wasn't it? Besides, what woman didn't like to shop?

"Da-da," Will said.

"That's right. Dada. I'm your dad." Will babbled all the time and said "Dada" occasionally, but Brian didn't believe he had any idea what it meant. Faith said if he didn't he would soon, but Brian wasn't too sure of that. The kid must still miss his mom, though he did seem happier since Faith had come to take care of him. His face lit up whenever he saw her.

After Will was dressed, Brian took him into the den and put him by the coffee table. Will could pull himself to a standing position and walk around holding on to things now. Cruising, the books called it. Brian had a feeling when the kid started walking, he and Faith would have a hard time keeping up. Will got into enough trouble already just crawling.

Faith came in carrying Lily and an enormous diaper bag. "Did you remember a change of clothes for Will?"

"They're in his diaper bag." Along with half the contents of his room. "He needs new clothes. I think he's only got two pairs of pants that fit."

"I know. Lily needs some, too. I planned on shopping tomorrow. If you're working, Gail offered to keep both the children while I shop. The sale prices make it worth braving the crowds but there's no way I'd take the babies out in that."

Brian shuddered. He couldn't imagine anything worse than shopping on the day after Thanksgiving.

Faith set Lily down on a blanket and started folding up one of the playpens. "Ava said to bring both the playpens so we can put the babies down for a nap if they want a rest. She's set aside a couple of bedrooms for them to sleep in."

"Do you really think they'll sleep there? With—" he tried to count and gave up, "however many babies are going to be there?"

"Five, including Will and Lily. They're more likely to sleep if we bring them something to sleep in."

Just more crap to haul around, he thought, but he folded up the other playpen and stowed them both in Faith's car. He still hadn't gotten around to buying another vehicle. Maybe he could do it over the long weekend.

"How many people are supposed to be here today?" he asked Faith as they went up the walk. He knew she'd been talking to Ava, so he figured she'd have an idea. "There sure are a lot of cars."

"Ava said thirty or more, including all the kids. They've invited some other people besides family, but I'm not sure who."

If someone had told him even six months ago that he'd be spending Thanksgiving with all these people in a scene of unparalleled domesticity, he'd have run screaming in the opposite direction. Come to think of it, he still might.

Certain no one would hear a doorbell, he opened the door and they stepped into the madhouse. People were everywhere, children were running around screaming and laughing, and one of the dogs came running up to him and planted its paws on his chest. Princess was Ava's overexuberant Lab mix. He petted her, discouraged her from licking Will in the face and made his way into the living room with Faith and Lily by his side.

His mother and her husband, Walt, were the first to greet them. Brian and Walt shook hands and then his mother enveloped him in a hug. "I'm so glad to see you, Brian. And my latest grandchild."

She held out her arms and Brian put Will into them. "Will, meet your grammy."

Walt and his mother had been out of the country

for several months and had only recently returned to the States. While Brian had told Lillian about his sudden fatherhood, she'd yet to meet her grandson.

"He's adorable, Brian. He looks just like you did at that age." She beamed at him fondly before turning to Faith. "And you must be Faith. What a beautiful baby. And her name is Lily? I'm Brian's mother, as I'm sure you've guessed. Lillian Monroe."

"Thank you. It's nice to meet you."

Faith seemed a little overwhelmed, looking around at all the people and activity. His mother must have noticed, too. "Would you like to bring Lily into the playroom? Roxy and Mel are in charge of that." She looked at Brian. "Is it all right if I take Will in there?"

"Sure. Have you seen Cullen yet?" he asked, knowing she'd been out of town since before Mark's youngest was born, as well.

"Not only seen him but changed him. I'm telling you, it's a grandmother's dream here today."

And what he once would have termed a single man's nightmare. Somehow it didn't seem so bad now. As Faith went off with his mother and the kids, he went to find Ava.

He found her in the kitchen with a number of people, including Mark's wife Cat, who was stirring something on the stove. Since Cat was a gourmet cook, she was always in charge of that aspect of the get-togethers. Brian shook hands with her brother,

Gabe Randolph, and his wife, Lana, and greeted Cole, Ava's stepson, who was headed outside with a football.

"Hey, Brian, do you want to play? We're getting a game up."

"I'll check in later. Thanks."

"It will be a while before dinner's ready," Ava said. "Get yourself something to drink," she told Brian, "and come talk to me. Where is that precious baby of yours?"

"Mom's got him. She said something about Roxy and Mel setting up a playroom."

"Bless them," Cat said as Brian pulled a beer from the refrigerator. "Roxy's having the time of her life with all the babies. And there are soon to be more, isn't that right, Gabe?"

Gabe put his arm around his wife and hugged her. "Absolutely. In about six months."

"That's wonderful. Congratulations," Ava said, and hugged Lana and Gabe.

"Ava, can you keep an eye on this?" Cat asked, motioning to the stove. "I'll be back in a minute."

"They should call it Baby City, not Aransas City," Brian said to Ava when the Randolphs had left the room and they were sitting at the kitchen table. "I've never seen so many babies in my life."

"That's not saying much, since before Will, you ran from every child under the age of ten."

"True." He grinned and took a sip of his beer. "That sure changes when you become a parent."

"Jack and I are hoping we'll find out what that's like for ourselves soon."

He stared at his sister. She'd told Mark she couldn't have children. Which could only mean… "You and Jack are adopting a baby? No kidding?"

She nodded, that blissful expression that women get when they talk of babies settling on her face. "We finished the paperwork last week. Now we just have to wait until they call us."

"That's great, Ava."

"There was a time I thought I'd never be a parent. But Jack changed my life. And even though Cole's a teenager, I've had him to practice on," she said and laughed.

"It seems to me that babies are a lot different from teenagers."

"I'm sure you're right." Ava peered at him closely. "So how are you doing with Will? The truth, not just the line you feed everyone."

"Better. Since Faith's been with us, he's stopped crying constantly. And sometimes I think he's actually starting to like me." He was a good kid. He'd taken to sitting in Brian's lap and snuggling against him while Brian read the paper. He seemed even happier when Brian read stories to him, which he'd been trying to do every night.

"I'm sure he loves you, Brian," Ava said and patted his hand.

Brian wasn't, but he kept his mouth shut.

"I'm so glad it's working out for you and Faith," Ava continued. "I don't know her very well but she seems so sweet. And Gail says it's obvious she's crazy about Will."

"She is sweet," he said. Very sweet. Pretty. Sexy. *Damn it, he had to get rid of these thoughts.*

"What's with the funny look? You're not thinking about—" She broke off as Faith came into the kitchen and the moment was lost.

Good. He didn't need a lecture about how he should keep his hands off his son's nanny. Like he didn't know that.

Later, he wound up squeezed onto the sofa beside Maggie Barnes while they ate dinner. Maggie was with the Aransas City police department, though she wasn't on duty today. "How's your little boy doing?" she asked. "He sure was screaming when I pulled you over."

"He spent about the first week with me crying all the time but he's calmed down now. He's doing all right." He looked around and spied his mother with Will on her hip talking to Mark, Cat and the baby. "I don't think my mom's let go of him since we got here."

"I can't blame her. He's a cutie."

"Is that why you only gave me a warning?" he asked, falling into an easy flirtation. Maggie was a very attractive redhead. She might be just the person to take his mind off of a certain blonde. He turned his head and saw Faith seated some distance away. She had Lily in her lap and a guy someone had mentioned was a single friend of Jack's seated beside her, trying to ply her with food and drink.

"Could be," Maggie said, smiling. "Or I might have just been in a good mood that day."

He and Maggie continued to talk. Brian tried to ignore Faith and her newfound friend, but without much success. Now the guy was holding Lily so Faith could eat. Didn't the joker know not to hold the baby like that? What if she fell off his lap? Why would Faith let some strange guy hold Lily?

Disgusted, he focused on the woman beside him. "Are you off duty tomorrow night? Or Saturday night?"

"Why?"

"Have dinner with me. You pick the night, whenever you're off."

A smile played around her mouth. "I like you, Brian. You're a nice guy."

"I sense a *but* coming on."

"I'm a cop. Which means I notice things. And one of the things I noticed while you've been sitting here flirting with me is the pretty blonde with the baby over there who keeps staring at you when she thinks you're not looking at her. And I also noticed that you, my friend," she tapped him on the knee, "keep staring at her when you think she's not looking at you."

Brian started to deny it but Maggie laughed and shook her head. "I make it a policy not to date a man who's hung up on another woman. So, no, I'll have to take a pass."

"The pretty blonde is my son's nanny. I'm not interested in her. Not like that."

"Just keep trying to convince yourself of that. The eyes don't lie." She got up and smiled at him. "Cheer up, Brian. Like I said, she's been checking you out, too."

He looked at Faith across the room and her eyes met his. She flushed and turned away, back to the man she'd been talking to for the past half hour. Maybe Maggie was right. Was Faith interested in him? And if she was, what was he going to do about it?

CHAPTER NINE

FAITH WOKE WITH A START, her heart pounding. She sat still for a moment wondering what had awakened her and then she heard it again. A baby crying.

"Mama, Mama," Will shrieked.

She grabbed her robe and threw it on before rushing to Will's room. Brian was there already, had taken Will out of his crib and was cuddling the sobbing child against his bare chest.

"You're okay," she heard Brian say as Will turned his wet cheek into the curve of his father's neck. "Don't worry. Daddy's here," he murmured. Will quieted, drawing in a deep shaky breath as Faith reached their side.

It was the first time she'd heard Brian refer to himself as Daddy and it touched her. She put a soothing hand on the baby's back and patted him. "Poor little guy. Do you think it was too much excitement today?"

"No. I think he still misses his mother." Will hiccuped and nestled closer to his father. Brian's eyes met hers in the dimly lit room. "And I know exactly how he feels."

She started to ask him what he meant but then heard Lily fussing. "Let me see to her. I'll just be a minute."

Lily had fallen back asleep by the time she reached her room. Faith caressed her head, tempted to pick her up, but she knew she'd wake her if she did. Love flooded her as she gazed at her baby. The perfect rosebud mouth, her chubby hand resting by her cheek. It no longer bothered her that Lily's father had left. He'd given her a precious gift in her baby girl and Lily was the only thing that mattered now.

She returned to Will's room and saw Brian putting him in his crib. "No more bad dreams, Will," he murmured, stroking the baby's head as she had Lily's only moments before.

It was as sweet a scene as she'd ever seen. As endearing as watching Brian comfort his son earlier. "You're getting to be a pro."

He looked at her and smiled. "Hardly. I have a long way to go."

She shook her head. "No, you don't. You're good with him. He loves you."

"Do you really think so?"

He sounded so uncertain, it broke her heart. "I know he does. And you love him."

He was quiet for a long moment, his hands on the

crib rail as he watched his son sleep. "I wasn't sure I could. At first I didn't know what I felt for him. I was afraid I might be like my father. That bastard never loved anyone in his life. Least of all his children."

The words were spoken softly but that only made them more chilling. "You sound very sure of that."

"Believe me, I am. He left when I was six. I prayed every night for a year that he'd never come back. Thank God he didn't."

"Did he—" she hesitated but then decided she'd ask him. "Did he abuse you? Is that why you wanted him gone?"

Brian shrugged. "Not physically. Not me. But Ava…he beat her so badly she ran away and we didn't see her for more than twenty years. We thought she was dead. That's on his head."

"I'm so sorry. That must have been awful for all of you." She'd heard bits and pieces of the story and knew that Ava had only recently reunited with her siblings. But she hadn't imagined anything so horrifying.

"Yeah, especially for Ava," he said grimly. "After she left, he didn't physically abuse the rest of us. No one knows why. But he had other ways of making us miserable. He was a mean, selfish son of a bitch who liked to play mind games with us."

"I'm sorry you had to go through that. No child should have to live with abuse. Of any kind."

"At least I only had to live with him for six years. Mark and Ava weren't that lucky."

She thought it spoke volumes that he felt fortunate to have lost his father at such a young age. She didn't know what to say so she simply waited for him to continue.

"It's funny. When my mother left us, I prayed every night she would come back. It had worked with my father, so I thought for sure praying would work with her. But she never came back. I finally decided that God must answer only one prayer and since He'd kept my father away, I was out of luck with my mother."

"I didn't realize... Your mother was at Thanksgiving with your family today."

He glanced at her before returning his gaze to his sleeping son. "We reconciled several years ago. But when I was eleven and Jay was twelve, she left us with Mark. She just dumped us on him and never came back. Mark was twenty-one and fresh out of college. But he never complained about having us, not to Jay nor to me. He worked his butt off to support us."

That nice woman she'd met earlier that day had abandoned her children? Had given them to their barely adult brother to raise? How in the world could she have done that? And how had they all forgiven her?

Brian looked at her. Her horror must have been written on her face because he said, "No, she's not a monster. She was sick. Clinically depressed. She went into a hospital, so she left us for Mark to raise. But she didn't tell us that. We all thought she just didn't want us anymore. She was hospitalized for two years. After she got out, she thought we were better off without her, because she didn't believe we could forgive her for abandoning us. When she remarried, her second husband talked her into trying to reconcile with us."

"Oh, Brian, how terribly sad."

He didn't look at her, continued to talk. "I was eleven. I thought I was tough until that happened. But I cried every night for months. I missed her so much. I hadn't known I could miss anyone like that. Jay knew but he didn't say anything. I guess he had his own fears to deal with. And his own tears."

"You were a little boy who'd lost his mother. Of course you weren't tough."

He shook his head and said softly, "When I first got Will he cried all the time for his mama. Like tonight, only worse. Nothing I did helped. And whenever he cried like that, those heartbroken, desolate sobs, I remembered crying for my mom." His hands tightened on the rails. "I felt like I was eleven all over again. Abandoned. Alone. Afraid."

She didn't know what to say so she simply put her hand over his and squeezed. She couldn't speak anyway, around the lump in her throat.

"It's been twenty years since that happened. I thought I'd dealt with it years ago. But hearing Will cry for his mother, it gets to me."

"Of course it does. It tears at anyone's heart to hear a baby cry for his mother."

"It's worse for Will than it was for me. His mom is dead. He'll never have the chance to reconcile with her. At least I had that."

But Will wouldn't remember his mother. Brian had lived with the memories and the loss for longer than Will would ever have to. "Will is lucky to have you." She wanted to take Brian in her arms and comfort him but she couldn't. That would be a huge mistake, just as allowing herself to feel too close to him now would be a mistake.

He half smiled at her. "Sorry to get so sentimental. That's not really my style."

"I know." He'd shared something very private with her and she guessed he didn't often do that with a woman. Possibly never. "Do you think that's why you don't trust women? Because of your mother?"

"I trust women."

"You trust them to leave you. You told me yourself you've never had a serious relationship and you're thirty-two years old. Most people have had at least one serious relationship by that point in their life."

"I said I'd never lived with a woman or been

married. I never said anything about not having relationships."

"But it's true, isn't it?"

He looked down at their hands, resting together on the crib railing. Realizing her hand still covered his, she hastily snatched it away. His lips curved into a smile.

"Yeah, it's true. To date, my longest relationship has lasted two months."

"Don't you ever want more? Haven't you ever thought that you're missing out on something?" she asked.

"Before I had Will I can honestly say it never crossed my mind. But now that I'm a father...I don't know. I just don't know." He turned toward her. "Pretty deep conversation for the middle of the night."

He was wearing sweat pants and nothing more, a fact she'd been aware of since she'd walked in the room. She'd seen Brian without his shirt before. For brief periods, which she carefully tried to never think about. But, oh, Lord, the man had some chest and it was right there in front of her, close enough to touch. A broad chest with abs that looked hard as a rock. She wanted to run her hands over those beautiful muscles, feel them ripple. *You idiot,* she told herself. She could fall for him in a heartbeat and he'd break her heart just like Peter Bruce had done.

Peter, who she'd never talked about. Not with

anyone. But she wanted to with Brian. She didn't know why, only that she wanted to share something that mattered with him, as he had with her.

"You can say things in the middle of the night that you wouldn't at other times."

He nodded. "Barriers are down. It's dark, it's quiet." After a few seconds of silence, Faith began.

"Peter, Lily's father, had told me he wanted to marry me. But it was a lie. When I found out I was pregnant, he said the baby—if there was one— wasn't his. He accused me of sleeping with other men. Instead of being angry, I crumpled. I was devastated. And you know what the worst of it was?"

"No. But being left high and dry when you're pregnant has to be right up there."

"That was bad. But the worst thing was my response. I hate that hurt, not anger, was my first reaction to the way Peter had treated me. My only reaction that he saw."

"Did you love him?"

"Yes. And I believed he loved me. Until I told him I was pregnant. Then it was painfully obvious he didn't and never had."

"He was a fool. You would never cheat on a man you loved."

"You can't know that."

"Sure I can. I know your character. You're so honest you'd get in the car and drive back to the store if you got home and found they'd given you too much change. A woman like you wouldn't cheat."

"No, I wouldn't. And I know Peter didn't really believe I had. He just said it so he didn't have to take responsibility. To justify leaving me."

"Do you still love him?"

"No. But I don't regret it, either. Not any of it. I have Lily and she's worth everything I went through and more."

He reached out and touched her hair, as he had one other time. He stood close to her, so close she could feel the warmth radiating from his body. If she stretched out her arm, she could run her hand over all those lovely muscles.

His hand slipped beneath her hair to the back of her neck.

She felt as if she were in quicksand and sinking fast. Unable to move, she gazed at him.

"So sweet," he said as he rubbed his thumb over her mouth, very gently. Very slowly. "God, you're sweet."

She couldn't speak. She just looked at him and willed him to kiss her. It would be a mistake. A huge mistake and yet she thought she'd die if he didn't kiss her.

She leaned toward him. Closer still. He cupped her face in his hands and lowered his head, stopping when their lips were only inches apart to stare into her eyes. *Kiss me,* her mind whispered.

But instead, he dropped his hands and turned and walked out of the room without a backward glance.

Faith sucked in a breath. He'd wanted to kiss her. She'd seen it in his eyes, felt it in his touch. She hadn't mistaken his intention. And she couldn't have appeared more receptive if she'd had Kiss Me stamped on her forehead.

She should be glad he'd had the sense to leave. To walk away from the temptation. He'd saved them both from making a massive mistake. But she wasn't glad. Not even one little bit.

BRIAN LEANED HIS BACK against his bedroom door and rubbed his hands over his face. God, he'd been so close to kissing Faith. Even now, he could almost taste her. He knew without a doubt she'd taste every bit as sweet as she was. He should have done it. Taken that beautiful mouth and kissed her like he'd been wanting to for weeks. One kiss wouldn't have hurt anyone.

Except he wouldn't have stopped with a kiss and he knew it. He didn't just want to kiss Faith, he wanted to make love with her. Long, slow, sweet love. Or fast and wild and crazy love. Or both.

It's just hormones, he thought. And no wonder. He'd been living with the woman and celibate for weeks now. It didn't help that she smelled so good, that soft, yet sexy scent that was uniquely hers. And it sure as hell didn't help that she'd grown so pretty. He'd seen her in the mornings, without makeup and wearing an old pair of sweats and he'd still thought she looked good.

He didn't want to hurt Faith. Her baby's father had already hurt her enough for one lifetime. And Brian knew that once he made love to her it would be the beginning of the end for them. He wasn't a forever kind of guy and Faith…she was definitely a forever kind of woman.

Will needed her. Brian needed her. But as his son's nanny, not as a lover.

He needed to date other women. Hell, he needed to get laid. Once he did he'd stop thinking about Faith and obsessing about how much he wanted to kiss her. How much he wanted to make love to her.

Wouldn't he?

CHAPTER TEN

BRIAN'S CELL PHONE rang when he had just finished up with a prospective client in Port Aransas the day after Thanksgiving. Checking caller ID, he saw that it was Faith and frowned. She never called him when he was working. Never. She was supposed to be shopping. Maybe she'd had car trouble. He walked out of the business office and into the hallway of the dental clinic and flipped open his phone.

"Faith, what is it?"

"I'm sorry to bother you while you're working, Brian, but I thought you'd want to know. I know why both the babies were fussy last night."

"What's wrong?"

"They have the stomach bug."

Stomach bug? "You mean they're throwing up?" That wasn't good. Not good at all.

"Afraid so. I wanted to warn you. These viruses are very contagious and you haven't—"

"I'll be there in twenty minutes." Ignoring her protest, he snapped the phone shut and sprinted to his car. Both babies were sick. He didn't know anything about sick kids. Hell, he didn't know anything about healthy kids. What if Faith was wrong and it wasn't just a virus? What if something serious was wrong with the kids?

By the time he reached home, he was a wreck, convinced the babies had some dire disease and for some ridiculous reason, Faith hadn't wanted to worry him.

"Faith!" he shouted as he walked in. "Where are you?"

She came into the den carrying Lily. "For heaven's sake, stop shouting. Will's just gone back to sleep."

He went to see for himself. Will was flushed, but he was sleeping, though fitfully. Brian put his palm on the baby's forehead and thought he felt warm, but what the hell did he know? Leaving the door ajar so he would hear Will if he woke, he headed back to the den to talk to Faith.

"I think Will has a fever. Does Lily have a fever?" He put his hand on Lily's forehead. "She feels warm. Have you taken her temperature? Did you take Will's? What was it?" Why was Faith standing there staring at him as if he'd lost his mind? "What?"

"Brian, calm down."

"Calm down? Are you nuts?" He paced away a few steps and whirled back to her. How could she be so calm? Wasn't she worried? "Have you called

Jay? Where the hell is he? This is his nephew and Lily we're talking about. He can damn well get his butt over here and examine them."

"Of course I haven't called the doctor. The clinic is closed, for one thing. It's a virus, Brian. Children get them all the time. I've given them some medicine I had from when Lily was sick before and they're already doing better."

"Better? Have you looked at them? They obviously feel terrible." Lily was as flushed as Will had been and fussing against her mother's shoulder. How could Faith say they were better?

"Well, they're sick." She patted Lily's back and bounced as she talked. "Naturally they don't feel well. Lily's had this virus before and you have to be careful they don't get dehydrated but—"

Ignoring her, he flipped open his cell phone and speed dialed Jay. "You need to come over here right now," he said as soon as Jay picked up. "And bring your doctor bag with you."

"What's wrong? Are you sick?"

"Not me. Will and Lily are both sick. You need to come over," he repeated.

"What are their symptoms?"

"Symptoms? What the hell does that matter? They're sick. Get your butt over here right now, Jay."

Faith took the phone from him and put it to her ear. "They have a stomach virus, Jay. I've given them the medicine you gave me for Lily when she had it before. They seem better. I don't think you need—"

Brian jerked the phone out of her hand. "If you're not over here in five minutes I'm coming to get you and it won't be pretty."

Jay had the gall to laugh. "All right, I'm coming. But settle down, Brian. It's probably just a stomach bug. One's been going around."

"What the hell does he know?" Brian muttered as he shut the phone.

FORTUNATELY, it didn't take Jay long to get there. Brian was seriously in danger of a meltdown, and Faith had her hands full trying to calm him down. It didn't help matters when Lily threw up again. She'd thought Brian was going to faint.

"Thank God," Brian said when he opened the door for his brother. "What took you so long?" Not waiting for an answer, he continued, "Will's in his room. He's asleep, but I want you to go ahead and look at him. Or maybe you should take care of Lily first. She just got sick again."

Jay put his hand on Brian's shoulder. "Brian, he's going to be all right. Both of them are. Okay?"

"How do you know? You haven't even seen Will and you've barely glanced at Lily." Eyes wild, he ran his hands through his already disordered hair. "What if they need to go to the hospital?"

Jay turned to Faith. "How long has he been like this?"

She knew he was talking about Brian, not Will. "Since I called him and told him they were sick." She checked her watch. "About forty-five minutes ago."

"Why don't I take a look at Lily, since she's awake. Let's bring her to her room, Faith."

Brian started to follow but Jay stopped him. "Go do something useful, Brian. Make some tea or something. Faith and I can see to Lily without your help."

"Well, you're getting my help whether you like it or not. Didn't I tell you she just threw up again? That baby is sick—all you have to do is look at her to know that—and so is Will. Isn't there a shot of something you can give—"

Brian was still arguing when Jay shut the door in his face. Jay looked at Faith and shook his head. "Good God, I've never seen him like this. What's he going to do if Will ever gets really sick?"

She hoped they never had to find out. "It's his first experience. I was pretty hysterical the first time Lily got sick. You had to calm me down."

"You did fine. First-time mothers are understandably nervous about their children."

Faith put Lily on the changing table and watched as Jay examined her.

"I'll cut him some slack since he's a first-time father. They don't always do well, either."

"He's scared. He loves Will so much. More than he realized, I think."

Jay glanced at her and seemed about to say something but apparently thought better of it. "Well, you called it," he said a few minutes later. "She has a little bit of a temperature. You can give her a lukewarm bath but the medicine you gave her should take effect soon. I've brought some more, too, in case you need it."

"Thanks. I was going to ask you for another prescription. I don't have much left, just enough for a couple of doses."

"I have some samples. You know the drill with a virus. The major concern is dehydration, but if it's a mild case and the meds are working, that shouldn't be a problem. You can give them an electrolyte solution, though. Do you have any?"

"Yes. I always keep some on hand. I'll call if I think there's a problem." And Brian would undoubtedly call him before that. "Thanks for coming over. It was kind of you."

"Are you kidding? I thought Brian was coming through the phone after me."

Faith laughed but she had to agree with him.

"We'd better go see about Will before Brian loses it completely. Let me wash up and I'll be right there."

When they opened the door Brian was leaning against the wall with his arms crossed over his chest and a grim look on his face. "How is she?"

"She has a virus," Jay said and went into the bathroom between the children's bedrooms.

"That's informative. Thanks for nothing." He walked into Will's room and Faith followed, carrying Lily. As soon as he saw his father, Will stood up in his crib crying and held out his arms. Brian picked him up, cradling him against his chest. "Poor little guy."

Thank goodness he hasn't thrown up again, Faith thought. She didn't think Brian could take it.

When Jay came in, he said, "Brian, why don't you take Lily back to her room and let Faith help me with Will?"

"No. I'm not leaving him." Will's chubby arms went around his father's neck as if in agreement.

Jay studied him a moment, then shrugged. "All right, but no more getting hysterical."

"I'm not hysterical. I'm concerned about the kids. Is that a crime?"

Jay looked at him and smiled sympathetically. "No, of course not. You know I'd tell you if this were something serious, right?"

Brian frowned. "I guess. They're just so little. And I've never seen a sick baby before. It's freaking me out."

"It's scary when your kids are sick, whatever their age. Why don't you put Will down on the changing table and let me check him over?"

Brian did as Jay asked but he stood right beside him, interjecting questions and making suggestions about what Jay should do, which Jay managed to ignore without seeming to. Faith wondered at Jay's patience but she figured he was accustomed to a lot of this sort of parental behavior in his practice. Not to mention, Brian was his brother and obviously scared to death.

Finally the ordeal came to an end and Jay allowed Brian to gather Will into his arms. "He has a virus, just like Faith thought," he told him. "I've given her the medicine and she knows how to administer it. I suggest you let her. You can start them on an electro-lyte solution, just little sips for now, but Faith knows all this. Listen to her, okay? The medicine makes them sleepy and sleep is the best thing for them right now."

Still holding Will, Brian sat down in the rocker. "That's it? That's all you're going to do?"

"That's all I can do right now. These viruses are usually short-lived. Twenty-four hours at most. But call me if either of them gets worse and I'll come right over."

"You're sure it's not serious?"

He looked so worried Faith wanted to hug him. Good thing she had her hands full and couldn't.

Jay smiled. "They'd have to be a lot sicker before I'd call it serious. Will and Lily are going to be all right in no time."

Faith walked Jay out while Brian stayed with Will. "Would you mind terribly coming back over in the morning? I'm sure it would set Brian's mind at rest."

"No problem. Poor guy. Kids have a way of wrapping their fingers around our hearts, don't they?"

"Yes, they do." And so, she was forced to admit to herself, did Brian. She was wading in some very treacherous water.

Lily had fallen asleep, so once Jay was gone, Faith took her to her room and put her to bed, hoping the worst of the illness had passed. In Will's room, she found Brian just as he'd been when she left, sitting in the rocker holding his son.

"Looks like he's asleep," she said softly. "Do you want me to put him to bed?"

"Not yet. I'll hold him awhile." Their eyes met and a corner of his mouth lifted. "You think I'm a moron, don't you? Because I flipped out over a virus."

"No. I think you love your son very much and you were scared."

"I care about Lily, too."

"I know you do." He'd been as hysterical about Lily as he had been about Will. How could she not fall for a man like him?

"How do you do it, Faith? You just took it in stride. You had two sick kids on your hands and you coped with them like you handle this kind of thing every day."

"I've had practice. Not with two of them at the same time, but with sick babies in general. Lily was sick a lot when she was in day care full-time. I told you that. The first time…I thought I would go nuts with worry and fear. I might have if it hadn't been for Jay. He's very soothing. I guess he has to be in his line of work."

Brian was watching his sleeping son. "Will turned to me. He looked at me like he knew I'd help him and he held out his arms to me. He's never done that before."

"I told you last night. He loves you."

Brian rose and laid Will down in his crib. "About last night—" he began.

"Don't, Brian. Just…let it go. Okay?" Because if they talked about what had almost happened, she wasn't sure what she'd do. Blurt out her growing feelings for him, most likely, and that would be a disaster.

"All right." He studied her for a long, intense moment. "But I don't think we can avoid this forever."

"Yes. We can." She sounded positive but she was anything but. She was determined not to go down that road, though. That road, she suspected, would lead to worse heartbreak than she'd already experienced.

Brian wasn't for her and it was time she remembered that. Past time.

CHAPTER ELEVEN

BY MORNING the babies were almost back to normal, but Brian wasn't. He couldn't remember ever being so scared or feeling such an absolute lack of control over a situation. Not since he was a child, anyway.

Faith assured him the babies were fine, though she was still feeding them that electrolyte stuff, he noticed. But she insisted she was perfectly capable of taking care of them, so he planned to go back to the dental clinic and start putting in the new system. The dentist had wanted him to work on it while the clinic was closed for the holiday, and since Brian was happy to have the job, he'd agreed.

When he went to tell the kids and Faith goodbye, he couldn't find Faith. Will was playing happily in his playpen but Lily was fussing in hers, so he got her out and discovered why she was crying. Her diaper was dirty.

"Let's go get your mom," he told her. Just because he knew how to change a diaper didn't mean he wouldn't avoid it when possible.

He tapped on Faith's bedroom door. Lily pulled on his ear and chortled happily, apparently having forgotten all about any discomfort. "Faith, are you in there?" She didn't answer so he opened the door and found her bathroom door closed. "Are you all right?" he asked, knocking there.

"Give me…a minute," she said.

Five minutes later, he was still waiting and Lily was fussing again, so he resigned himself to changing her, then put her in her playpen and went back to Faith's room. He sat on her bed and waited for her to come out of the bathroom.

"You have the virus, don't you?" he asked when she finally emerged. Her complexion was pasty white and she looked like she felt terrible, so he didn't really need the verbal confirmation.

"No, I'm fine. You go on to work."

"Faith, you're sick. You can't take care of Will and Lily like this."

"I'm not sick. Just a little—" she broke off, rushed back into the bathroom and slammed the door.

"Right. You're not sick at all. You're healthy as a horse."

He left the room and called Jay. "Faith has it now."

"Not surprising. These bugs are extremely contagious. You'll probably get it, too."

"No, I won't. I can't. I have to take care of the babies. Can you tell me exactly what and how much

I'm supposed to feed them? Faith isn't up to talking right now." He made notes about what Jay told him and hung up. He knew their schedule, more or less, so he could make do on that end. Besides, how hard could it be? Faith looked after both of them all the time with no problem. He knew what he was doing with Will now. Surely it wouldn't be that bad taking on Lily, too.

He called the dentist to cancel, assuring him he'd make it in the next week, after hours if he wanted. By then both babies were crying so he went to them.

An hour later, he'd decided that any woman who could do what Faith did every day was Super-woman. One of the babies was always hungry, dirty, wet or just plain fussy. He'd no sooner get one of them settled down than the other would start up. And when they were both cranked up and wailing in tandem, he wanted to pull his hair out.

He managed to keep Will occupied by giving him a wooden spoon, which he banged on the coffee table. Over and over and over. Not very good for the coffee table or Brian's head, but hey, it kept the kid busy and happy so Brian could feed Lily some of that electrolyte stuff.

Several hours later, after he'd miraculously managed to put both kids down for a nap and was sitting on the couch in a stupor, Faith came into the den. She looked pitiful, as wiped out as anyone he'd ever seen.

"I'm feeling a little better. I'm sorry you've had to take care of the babies."

"I didn't mind. You don't look like you feel any better."

She was wearing her glasses and sweats. Her face was still pinched and white and her eyes glassy. She looked to him like she could hurl at any moment.

"Well, I do." She sat in the easy chair and sighed. "I think I'm over the worst of it now, if you want to go back to work. I had some water and ginger ale and feel almost human again."

Brian laughed. Yeah, he would go off and leave her with both babies when she obviously felt like hell. "Don't be ridiculous, Faith. Go back to bed."

She pouted. He'd have thought it was funny if she clearly hadn't felt so bad. "You shouldn't have to take care of the children. That's what you hired me for. And especially not Lily. She's not even your child."

"Are you saying you don't trust me to take care of the kids?"

"Of course I trust you. But they're my responsibility."

"Today they're not. Faith, go to bed. Get some sleep. You'll feel a lot better after you do."

She pouted some more but she eventually

dragged herself off to bed. *Just call me Mr. Mom*, Brian thought as he headed to Will's room to answer his cry.

Who would have believed six months ago that Brian Kincaid, confirmed bachelor, would be taking care of two babies under a year old? And doing a pretty damn decent job of it, too.

"DID YOU WANT TO HAVE a party for Will's first birthday?" Faith asked Brian Tuesday night. They'd put both babies to bed and Faith was cleaning up after dinner. "Isn't his birthday Thursday? If we're going to have a party we need to get it planned."

Brian put down the newspaper he was reading. "You're supposed to have a party for a one-year-old? He won't know it's his birthday."

"But you will. If you want to do something simple, we could have your family over for cake and presents after work. Maybe order pizza." She picked up the sponge and began wiping down the stove top.

"My whole family together in this house? Remember Thanksgiving? It'll be a zoo."

"No, it will be fun. You'll see. And we aren't talking about having nearly as many people as were at your sister's house."

Just half that many. But Faith seemed excited and obviously wanted to do something for the kid. "Well…okay. If you think we should, then let's do it." His son's first birthday. How mind-boggling was that?

"Good. Are you going to get his present or do you want me to pick something out?"

"I'll do it. But I could use some help. Why don't we go shopping on Thursday when the babies are in Mothers' Day Out?"

"All right. I can pick up some decorations then, too. This will be so fun. I love parties. And the grocery store has good cake. I can order that over the phone tomorrow."

"Cat won't like that. She usually makes the cakes for family birthdays. And hers are great." He knew because he'd happened to be in town for Jay's birthday one time and had a piece of the cake she'd brought over.

"Your sister-in-law has an infant. She might not be up for baking cakes."

Bummer, he hadn't thought of that. "I'll talk to Mark and if she doesn't want to bake it, you can order one. So, is there anything else we need to do?"

"Not that I can think of." She put the sponge down, picked up a pot and began drying it. "But I have a favor to ask you."

"Ask away."

"Can you take care of Will Friday night? Roxy said she'd mind Lily for me."

"You have a date?" He didn't know why he was

surprised. Except she hadn't been out since her date with Dr. Smooth and he'd thought she had decided not to go out with him again. "I thought you blew off that guy."

"Oh, it's not with him." She stowed the pot below the stove top, then started loading the dishwasher with the supper dishes. Every night that she cooked, he offered to help clean up, and every night, she turned him down. "The date is with someone else. I just met him today."

"Where did you meet him?" Not that it was any of his business but she *was* living with him. Taking care of his son. He had a right to some…curiosity about who she dated.

Faith turned and gave him a surprised look. "In the grocery store. The produce section." She laughed. "He asked me to pick out a cantaloupe for him. Why?"

"You're going out with a man you met in the grocery store? Over a cantaloupe? Isn't that kind of—" He broke off and searched for the word he wanted. *Stupid,* he thought, but didn't say it. "Isn't that kind of chancy?"

"No, why? He seemed perfectly nice. His name is Brent Walken. He owns a gym in Port Aransas and one in Rockport. Do you know him?"

"No, I don't know him and neither do you. He could be a creep. Or a pervert. Or married."

She stopped loading the dishwasher and turned

around, her hand on her hip. "He's not a creep or a pervert," she said, obviously peeved. "He's divorced and he says he's lived in Aransas City for ten years. And if you don't want to keep Will, just say so."

"Don't be st— ridiculous. Keeping Will isn't the problem. I just think you ought to be more careful about who you go out with. Hell, this dude could be a serial killer for all you know."

She laughed. "Maybe you should ask your police officer friend for a background check."

"What friend?" he asked blankly.

"You know, the redhead you were so chatty with on Thanksgiving."

"You mean Maggie Barnes? I hardly know her."

"You and she seemed awfully cozy sitting together on the couch." She turned back around. "It looked to me like you were hitting on her."

And why would Faith care if he had been? Unless, like Maggie had believed, she wanted him for herself. "I wasn't hitting on Maggie. I asked her out."

"Same thing."

"It isn't the same thing at all," he said, stung. "There's a big difference between hitting on a woman and asking her out for a date."

"Name one."

He couldn't think of one, which annoyed the hell out of him. "Never mind that. At least I didn't meet her in a grocery store, for God's sake."

She glared at him. "I hate to have to break the news to you but I'm perfectly capable of taking care of myself. I'm a grown woman with a child and I've been on my own for a long time now." She wagged her index finger at him. "*And* I can date whomever I damn well please without any input from my employer. All I want to know is if you'll take care of Will that night or if I need to get a babysitter for him, as well as Lily."

Her voice had risen with every word. He'd never heard Faith shout before, but then, he'd never seen her mad. He found it…fascinating. And a little bit of a turn-on to see mild-mannered, soft-spoken Faith McClain all worked up and bent out of shape.

Her employer. If he wasn't her employer he'd go over there and kiss her and make her forget all about…what's his name. But he *was* her employer so nothing like that was going to happen.

Not tonight, not ever.

"Of course, I'll take care of Will," he said irritably. "But I hope you don't regret this."

"I won't," she snapped.

"Fine." He picked up the paper and shook it out, even though he was way too pissed to read.

She banged around putting away the pots and pans and muttered something that sounded like *jackass*. Brian pretended to read the paper. A few minutes later, she said, "When are you going out with Maggie?"

He put the paper down and looked at her. He started to lie but decided that would make things way too complex and besides, she'd undoubtedly find out for herself at some point if he lied about that. From Maggie herself, if no one else. "I'm not. She shot me down."

"Oh. Why?"

Because she thinks I'm hung up on you. No how, no way was he going there. "How do I know? She's a woman. Sometimes they say yes, sometimes they don't. So what?"

"I'm sorry."

He shrugged. "No big deal. If at first you don't succeed, move on to the next one. I've got a date Saturday night with someone else." Which was still a lie but not one she would catch him in. He could get a date easily enough, but it wouldn't be with Maggie Barnes. Or Faith.

"You hadn't mentioned having a date Saturday," she said suspiciously.

"I'm mentioning it now."

"Is it with one of the casserole ladies?"

"No. I wouldn't date any of them. She works for my new client in Corpus Christi. She's Dr. Blair's receptionist."

"What's her name?"

He blanked on that, then picked one at random. "Virginia. Virginia Baker."

"I suppose she's beautiful. That's one of your requirements, isn't it?" She crossed her arms over her chest and leaned back against the counter. He couldn't be sure but he thought she was smirking.

"I wouldn't call it a requirement. But yeah, Virginia's a knockout," he confirmed. "Long, wavy black hair, ocean-blue eyes," he added, getting into the fantasy. "Tall. Curvy." He made an hourglass shape with his hands. "She used to model. Lingerie and stuff like that."

"She went from modeling to working as a receptionist? Why? Didn't she make a lot more money modeling?"

Dumb-ass, he thought. *You should have stopped while you were ahead.* "Did I say receptionist? Actually she's more like his executive secretary. She likes the hours better."

Faith clearly wasn't buying it. "Still seems strange to me, but whatever floats your boat."

"You quit your last job because of Lily. Maybe she had good reason to leave modeling."

"I didn't quit. I was fired."

He winced, feeling like a jerk for reminding her of losing her job. "Whatever. I didn't get all the details from her. A woman's work history isn't exactly high on my list of questions when I'm asking her out." And why in the hell were they discussing his imaginary date with an imaginary former model turned secretary? *Damn.* Executive assistant.

To make Faith jealous, that's why. How stupid was that? He didn't play games like this. He'd never needed to. But then, he'd never been stuck on a woman he couldn't have. Hell, he'd never been stuck on a woman he *could* have.

He *wasn't* stuck on Faith. He wanted to make love to her. That's all. Nothing like being stuck on her.

"Yes, I feel sure you're much *smoother* than that."

That was him. Brian Kincaid, the king of smooth, lying through his teeth. He couldn't even think of a decent comeback.

"I'm going to bed. I'll see you in the morning," Faith said and left the room.

Brian raked his hands through his hair. He couldn't continue to live with Faith like this and not lose his mind. He had to stop thinking about taking her to bed and the obvious way to do that lay in another woman's arms. He needed a date. He needed to get laid. And he really, really needed to forget about Faith McClain.

CHAPTER TWELVE

"Look, isn't this cute?" Faith handed Brian a stuffed pink hippo. "Feel how soft it is."

"Uh-uh." He handed it back. "No way. It's pink. You want me to give my son a girl toy? Where's the boy stuff?"

Faith curbed her exasperation. Who knew Brian would be such a perfectionist when it came to picking out a present for Will? They were at their third store, since he'd rejected everything in the first two. He'd at least allowed her to buy the decorations at the discount store, but insisted they try another store for the toys. At this rate they'd never finish in time to pick up the babies at Mothers' Day Out.

He'd found some upscale baby store in Corpus Christi with, in Faith's opinion, overpriced toys that they could have just as easily picked up at the discount store if he'd only been patient enough to look. But he'd found the Baby Palace on the Internet that morning and was convinced it would have what they needed.

Maybe the pink hippo was a little girlie. "There's no such thing as girl and boy toys," she said nonetheless. "You don't want him to be sexist, do you?"

Will's a boy. He ought to have something boys like to play with. Like this." He reached up to the top shelf and pulled down an enormous box that had a picture of a colorful garage with big plastic cars on it. "Yeah, this is more like it."

"That's a very good choice, sir," the salesclerk said, beaming at him. "You have discerning tastes. The StarBright garage is one of our bestsellers."

Faith rolled her eyes. Sheena, as her name tag read, was a curvaceous brunette who had latched on to them the minute they'd walked into the store. She'd obviously figured out Brian was a soft touch. When she'd assumed Faith was Brian's wife, he had quickly set her straight and ever since the woman had flirted with him shamelessly. Which he clearly didn't mind, since he flirted right back.

"All right, I'll take it," Brian told her. "Also the jack-in-the-box and the nesting cubes. And throw in that pink hippo, too."

"I thought you didn't want him to have a girlie toy?" Faith said.

"The hippo's for Lily." He turned back to the clerk. "And I need something for my nephew, too. He's about a year and a half, I think."

"I know just the thing."

"Are you getting these presents for Christmas?" Faith asked as Brian followed the clerk to another aisle. "I didn't realize you wanted to Christmas shop today."

"No, we don't have time. We'll have to save Christmas shopping for another day."

"Then why are you buying toys for Jason and Lily?"

"I don't want them to feel left out. Mel and Roxy and Cole are old enough not to care, but—" he broke off and smacked his forehead. "I can't believe I forgot about Mark's kids. I'd better get them something, too."

"Brian, it's just before Christmas. You'll be buying them all toys then."

"So I'll get them different ones for Christmas. That looks good," he said when Sheena dragged out a bright red push car. "I need three more toys," he added, and told her the genders and ages of his oldest brother's children.

"That's very generous of you," the clerk gushed before Faith could speak. "Your nieces and nephews will love these toys. And the pink hippo is adorable, isn't it? Do you want me to gift wrap all the presents?"

"Sure, why not?"

"Yes, why not, it's only money," Faith said sarcastically. She could hear the *ka-ching* of the cash register ringing in the woman's ears.

Brian's eyes were a beautiful, vibrant green that right now looked at her with some amusement. "Do you think Lily would like the hippo or not?"

"Of course she'd like it. She loves cuddly toys."

"Good. Ring everything up," he told Sheena. "You've been a big help. Thanks."

"Oh, it's been my pleasure. I'll ring these up before I gift wrap them and then bring you the receipt." She beamed again and left with the cart full of toys.

"Why are you so grumpy?" Brian asked Faith. "You've been snapping my head off all morning."

"No, I haven't. I just think it's a waste of money to pay for gift wrapping when I could do it at home for a lot less. Do you have any idea what they charge to gift wrap in a place like this?"

"I don't think a little gift wrap is going to break me." He studied her for a minute and she fought the urge to squirm. "Is there something else? Did the gym rat break your date?"

"No, he didn't. And don't call him that. I didn't sleep well last night, that's all."

"I didn't hear Will during the night."

"Lily was fussy," she improvised.

Lily had nothing to do with her restless night. Brian, on the other hand, had everything to do with it. She'd dreamed about him. About being in his arms and kissing him. About making love with him.

Sexy, sensual dreams. She'd never had those kinds of dreams in her life. Not about anyone, until now.

Damn it, what was she supposed to do when her subconscious mind betrayed her? She'd made another date, hadn't she? She was doing her best to ignore what she felt every time she looked at Brian. Every time she thought about him.

If Brian had been totally disinterested that would make her attempts easier. But he was fighting the attraction as much as she was. Remembering his reaction to her date she nearly laughed. If she didn't know better, she'd have thought he was jealous. Even so, he clearly didn't mean to do anything about it. Him and his supermodel date. Not that she'd believed him for a minute, but she didn't doubt that by now he had a real date with some bombshell.

Sheena came back with the gaily wrapped packages and after another few minutes of Brian and the woman flirting, they finally left.

Fortunately, Brian had bought a new car—a small SUV to drive the kids around in—and they were able to fit all the packages in the back of it.

"It was really sweet of you to buy Lily a toy." She hadn't been very appreciative, Faith thought guiltily. And Brian was good to her baby.

"Every little girl should have a pink hippo." He gave her the beguiling smile that went straight to her heart. "Make sure you don't lose those coupons

Sheena put in the bag. We'll need them for Christmas shopping."

"I'll get them out and put them in my purse." Even though it would take a pretty big discount to make these prices seem reasonable to Faith. She looked through the plastic bag and pulled out a wad of paper. Coupons and flyers of every description. Faith glanced at the one on top. *Oh, pu-leeze.* Picking it up, she waved it at Brian. "I wonder if this means she discounts her services, too."

He shot her a cocky grin. "Sheena's phone number?"

"How did you guess?"

"You really don't like her, do you? I thought she was nice."

"Nice? She was so obviously after you, I'm surprised she didn't strip naked in the toy aisle."

Brian burst out laughing. "Now that's an image that would not have entered my mind."

What was wrong with her? She never made catty remarks about other women. Well, almost never. Jealousy was not having a good effect on her.

WHEN BRIAN WALKED IN that afternoon, he'd thought he'd stepped into an explosion. He hadn't paid much attention when Faith had picked out the decorations, but judging from the kitchen, she'd decided on bears. Blue bears. With blue and white streamers and blue and white balloons and blue bears, bears, bears. Everywhere.

Will had liked them. His chubby little face had lit up when Brian carried him into the kitchen. He laughed and clapped his hands and reached for everything. He was soon sitting at the kitchen table in his high chair playing with a stuffed bear. A blue stuffed bear, of course.

Who knew Faith could be such a smart-ass?

"So what does it feel like to be the father of a one-year-old?" Mark asked him later in the evening after the pizza and cake had been demolished and all the presents opened.

They'd retreated to the kitchen in search of a little quiet, but they could still hear laughing and screaming from the other room. Roxy and Mel had organized some kind of game and one of the key elements seemed to be whoever was the loudest won.

"It's not as weird as it was at first. I don't wake up anymore wondering why there's a crying baby in my house. Or babies," he added reflectively. "And man, does Will have a temper sometimes. He must have gotten that from his mother."

Mark gave a crack of laughter. "I remember you as a baby. Trust me, he got it from his daddy."

Brian laughed but then turned sober. "It still scares the hell out of me to realize that I'm totally responsible for another person," he admitted. "A baby. But at least we have Faith to help us. I don't know what I'd do without her."

"You'd cope. But it's good you don't have to."

"Will's crazy about her." He motioned to the decorations. "The party and everything was her idea. She did it all. I don't know how she does everything she does. It took me days to recuperate after one day of taking care of the kids when she was sick."

"Sounds like she's a godsend, all right. And I'd never have thought of giving the other kids a toy, too. Faith had a good idea there."

"Hey, that was my idea. I read it in one of those books Cat and Gail gave me." He thought about Will's reaction to his new toys and smiled. "I wonder when Will's going to figure out he's supposed to play with those cars and not throw them at people." He rubbed the bridge of his nose. The kid was too young to have such a good arm.

"If he's like Max, it will be a long time. Speaking of toy cars, I'm sorry Miranda flushed one down the toilet. She learned that from Max. I swear, I was watching her but she can disappear faster than seems humanly possible."

"That's all right. We'll get the plumber out in the morning." He surveyed the kitchen. Cat had come through with the cake and what hadn't been eaten appeared to be spread around the room. Even on the ceiling. "Does it always look like this after a kid's party?"

"It gets worse," Mark warned. "Wait until he's older."

Faith came into the kitchen just then with Lily. "I need a bottle. I have to put her down. I think she's a little overstimulated."

Brian looked at the red-faced, wailing baby and thought so, too. Will would probably be impossible to get to sleep, as well. "I can hold her for you."

"Okay, but you asked for it." Faith passed Lily over to Brian and went to fix her bottle.

The baby's breath caught on a tremulous sigh. Suddenly quiet, she stared at Brian, her eyes big, blue and wet with tears. "It's okay, beautiful." He made a face at her and was rewarded with a smile. Encouraged, he tried another and she waved a dimpled hand in the air and laughed.

He glanced at his brother, who was grinning at him knowingly.

"What? She likes it when I make faces." He'd discovered that while Faith was ill. If Mark hadn't been there he'd have sung to her, which he'd also done that day he'd taken care of Lily and Will. But he couldn't sing in front of his brother and not feel like a fool. Come to think of it, he wouldn't sing in front of Faith, either, unless it was an emergency.

"Her bottle's ready," Faith said, coming to his

side. "You're a miracle worker. Thanks." She took Lily from him, cradled her and gave her the bottle. "There, now. Is that better?"

Brian smoothed a hand over the fine baby curls. He glanced up and saw Faith watching him, her eyes soft and brown and warm with pleasure. There was a dab of icing at the corner of her mouth. He wanted to put his mouth there and taste it, slide his tongue over those plump lips, slip it into that pretty mouth and…

He stopped himself middaydream, looked into Faith's eyes and saw the same desire reflected in their depths. Her lashes fluttered closed, she turned away and walked quickly out of the room with Lily in her arms.

Mark cleared his throat.

Crap. He'd completely forgotten his brother was in the room.

"You've fallen for her." It wasn't a question.

"For Faith? No, I haven't."

"Yes, you have. Not only for Faith, but for Lily, too."

Brian leaned back against the counter and gave him his most cynical smile. "Get real. You know me. Does that sound like me?"

"It doesn't sound like Brian the player. But Brian the father, I don't know about him."

"I'm the same person I was before I knew I was a father, Mark."

"I don't think so. I saw the way you looked at her, Brian. I saw how you looked at the baby. And I saw the way Faith looked at you. Are you sure you know what you're doing here?"

"I'm not doing anything. You're making a big deal out of nothing."

"Am I?"

"Look, she's great with Will and I like her. But there's nothing going on. She's not my type. Besides, she's my kid's nanny. Hands off, remember?"

"I remember," Mark said. "The question is, when she looks at you like that again, like you hung the moon, will *you* remember?"

CHAPTER THIRTEEN

"Oh, come on, Faith. One drink won't hurt you."

Faith eyed her date with dislike. "I already had a glass of wine. Why are you so anxious for me to drink more?" If he thought alcohol would make her easier, which she suspected he did, he had another think coming.

"Because you're the most uptight woman I've ever taken out. You need to loosen up."

Not in this lifetime. And not with this loser. "Look, Brent, why don't we call this a wash and you take me home?" She glanced around for the waitress but, not surprisingly, couldn't find her. A four-star restaurant it was not.

This made two dates for two that had been less than fun. Not a good start to getting back "out there." Was this all there was?

To be fair, her first date hadn't been as bad as this one, but she hadn't enjoyed it all that much, either. And Brian had cured her of wanting to date him again, when he'd implied the man was only out to seduce her. But that wasn't the real problem. No, the real problem was no man was going to measure up to the one she really wanted to be with.

Firmly, she turned her thoughts away from him. He was the reason she'd gone out with this guy in the first place. She was trying to forget about Brian, but instead she'd done nothing but think of him all night. Damn it.

But just because she had to forget about Brian didn't mean she had to endure Mr. Buff but Boring here. "Take me home, Brent," she repeated.

Half an hour later, she got in his car and breathed a sigh of relief. Damn Brian for being right. She should never have gone out with a man she'd met over produce. But no, she'd been determined to go so she could prove Brian wrong. Hah.

Glancing out the window she realized they were nowhere near the highway that went to Aransas City. "Where are you going? I thought you were taking me home."

He shot her an insufferable grin. "Relax, baby. Just one more quick stop and then I'll take you home." He winked. "Unless you want to come to my place instead."

"I'll pass. I don't want to go anywhere else. Please just take me home."

He scowled at her and kept driving in the same direction. Away from Aransas City. Nothing she said—and she said a lot—got through to him. Finally, he pulled into the parking lot of a seedy-looking bar named the Rusty Nail.

Oh, fun. Just what she wanted. To go to a dive with a complete jerk. "Are you crazy? I want to go home."

"One drink. Then I'll take you home."

She didn't believe him for a minute. But she didn't like the looks of the parking lot, so she decided to go inside and call a cab from there. Enough was enough. She pushed her door open, got out and stalked inside ahead of her would-be lover boy. She hoped Brian was asleep when she got home. She didn't want him to have a clue as to just how bad her date had turned out.

DAMN, TWENTY-ONE LOSSES in a row. That had to be a new record. Brian sighed and checked the time on the computer. Two minutes later than the last time he'd checked. Good God, he needed to get a life.

He got up, opened the door of his office and listened for the babies, but they weren't making a sound. Still exhausted from the party the night before, he figured, since they'd both been tired and cranky all day.

The TV was on in the den but all he heard was a low murmur of voices. Roxy was in there watching a movie she'd brought with her, some kind of comedy. She was babysitting Lily while Faith was out on her date.

Brian had met the guy when he came to pick up Faith. Not much to write home about in his opinion, but once the door closed behind them his niece had sighed and said he looked like McSteamy, whoever the hell that was. Some dude on a TV show he didn't think her parents knew she watched. Whatever. According to Roxy, the gym rat was hot.

He wondered if Faith thought so.

Roxy had asked him if he wanted to watch the movie with her after the babies went to bed, but he'd begged off, saying he had work to do on his computer. Some work.

God knows he needed to work. He had paperwork coming out his ears. He'd tried to take care of it but it just wasn't happening. Instead, he'd been playing Spider Solitare all night long, and losing. Probably because his mind really wasn't on the stupid computer card game.

He wondered if Faith was having fun. If she was steaming up the windows with the steamy gym rat. If she was letting the guy hold her, touch her… Shit, why torture himself? He ought to put Faith and what she might or might not be doing out of his mind.

He closed the door and walked to the window. Pushed aside the blind and peeked out, but since it was dark—and his office window faced the backyard—he couldn't see anything. He ought to turn his thoughts to Corinna. She of the amazingly supple and curvaceous body. Corinna, who, after he'd broken down and called her for a date for Saturday night, had intimated he could be in for a night of truly unforgettable sex. He'd decided to hell with a woman's brain. Faith had one and look where that had gotten him.

Playing Spider Solitaire on his computer on a Friday night waiting for the nanny to come home. Can you spell *loser?* he asked himself. With a capital *L.*

The phone rang, but he didn't bother to answer it. Roxy would have the cordless right beside her. Besides, it was probably Faith calling to check on Lily and he didn't want to talk to Faith right now.

A minute or so later Roxy tapped on the door. "Uncle Brian?"

"Come in," he called.

She walked in holding out the cordless phone. "Faith wants to talk to you." He took it from her and she added in a stage whisper, "She sounds funny."

"What's wrong?" he barked into the receiver.

"Nothing's wrong. Except…uh, I'm going to be a bit later than I'd planned. I'd told Gail I'd have Roxy back early and I won't be able to make it home for a while yet."

"Why?"

She floundered until he wondered if she'd ever spit it out. A disturbing thought occurred to him, but he dismissed it almost as soon as he had it. No way would Faith spend the night with some guy she barely knew.

Finally, she sighed and said, "I'm waiting for a cab. I'm not sure how long it's going to take and I'm in Corpus so even if one gets here it will be a while."

A cab? She'd called a cab? For an instant his mind blanked, then he saw red. "What did that sorry son of a bitch do to you?"

Roxy gasped and her eyes widened.

Damn, he'd forgotten she was there. "You didn't hear that," he told her, wishing she'd leave the room and knowing she wouldn't. "Faith, what happened? Are you all right? Is he drunk, is that the problem?"

"I'm fine. I just…needed a cab. I'll explain it when I get home. The cab's pulling up right now." She hung up before he could say anything else.

"What's going on, Uncle Brian?" Roxy asked, her eyes big.

"Trouble, that's what," he said grimly. Within minutes, the phone rang again and he answered. "I'm coming to get you," he said, before Faith could say anything.

"Thanks. I hate to ask, but I don't know what else to do. I feel like a fool but the cab driver won't bring me that far without the fare up-front and I don't have that much on me."

He paced away and turned his back to Roxy. "Where the hell are you?"

"At a club in Corpus. Let me go inside and ask the bartender for directions. I really don't know where it is."

A few moments later she gave him an address in a not-so-great part of town.

"I'll call Jay and have him come stay with Roxy and the babies and then I'll be there. Are you at the bar?"

"Yes. The bartender is very nice. He's the one who— Well, never mind. He's nice, though."

"Good. Just stay put until I get there. And don't, for God's sake, go outside again until I come in and get you." What was she doing in what was undoubtedly a dive? In that part of town, she'd get mugged or worse waiting for him outside.

He disconnected then dialed his brother immediately, hanging up again after Jay promised to come right over.

He looked up to find Roxy staring at him. "I guess you figured out from my end of the conversation that I have to go pick up Faith."

Roxy nodded, her eyes still huge. "Is Faith hurt, Uncle Brian?"

She'd better not be or her date was a dead man. But he didn't want to scare Roxy—no more than he already had. "I don't think so. She said she was fine."

"Then why do you have to go get her?" Roxy asked reasonably. "Is her date drunk? Is that why?"

He rubbed the back of his neck. Where was Jay? He was Roxy's stepfather; he should be the one explaining shit like this to the kid. "I'm not sure. Maybe. He might not be willing to give her the keys to drive home. Men do stupid things like that sometimes."

Roxy nodded wisely. "I know. My mom told me all about that and what I'm s'posed to do if that happens to me when I start dating."

"You're way too young to date." Didn't he have enough to worry about without thinking of his niece going off with some creep? In a car?

"I know. Mom says I can date at sixteen, but Jay and Daddy don't like that idea." She rolled her eyes and giggled. "They both said, 'absolutely not,' but Mom said we'd see." She shot him a mischievous glance. "I expect Mom will win, though. She usually does."

Brian barely repressed a shudder. "That's your parents' business. But if you ever get into trouble or a situation you can't handle, you call your dad or Jay or me and we'll come get you. Okay?"

"'Kay." She fell silent a moment, then asked curiously, "Are you gonna kick his ass, Uncle Brian?"

Brian laughed. The kid had ears like a bat. She'd probably heard his brother or her father say that when they didn't know she was listening. "That depends on what he did. But yeah, if he hurt Faith I'm going to kick his ass from here into next week."

THE DOOR TO THE BAR slammed open and a man stood silhouetted against the night. Faith sucked in a deep breath and let it out slowly. Brian. Looking like the ultimate romantic fantasy. All he lacked was the fiery steed. Tall, dark, dangerous…and mad as hell. It depressed her, but didn't surprise her that her first response to seeing him was a tsunami of pure, unadulterated lust.

And after the lust came embarrassment that she'd had to call him to come to her rescue.

His gaze zeroed in on her like a laser and seconds later, he stood in front of her. She reminded herself that it wasn't a crime not to have the fifty-buck cab fare she needed to get home. Raising her chin, she met his gaze head-on.

"Are you all right?" He managed to infuse the words with a wealth of meaning.

"I told you on the phone, I'm fine." *Thank God.* She pulled her jacket closer around herself.

"Where is he?" Faith simply stared at him. "The gym rat. Where is he?"

"Yo. You botherin' my girl there?"

"It's all right, Joe," Faith said hastily. "He's a friend of mine."

Joe looked Brian up and down, then shrugged. "You gonna take Faith home, man?"

Brian flicked the bartender a glance before fixing his gaze on her again. "Yeah. After I find someone."

Joe, a six-foot-five white man with a gold tooth to match the gold chains hanging around his neck, swabbed down the bar with a grimy rag. "If you're lookin' for the dude who was hassling her, you ain't gonna find him here. My bouncer threw that jackass out." He gave Brian a measured look. "Good thing, because if you think you're gonna bust up my bar, think again."

"No, of course he won't," Faith said. "Thank you so much, Joe." She slipped him a twenty, all she had on her. That was the last time she went on a date without at least fifty in cash. "You've been very kind."

He waved a hand. "Comes with the job, honey. But thanks for the tip."

Someone shouted for the bartender. "I'm busy, dip-wad," he yelled back. "Hold on to your panties." He sighed and shook his head. "Pretty lady, do me a favor and don't come back. You don't belong here."

"I know. Don't worry." She slid off the bar stool and stood. No, the Rusty Nail was definitely not her type of place.

Brian put his hand under her arm and propelled her to the door. "I'm sorry you had to come get me.

The cab driver absolutely refused to take me to Aransas City without the money up-front."

"The question is, Faith, why did you need a cab in the first place?" He'd stopped in the doorway and stood there like the Rock of Gibraltar, clearly not budging until she answered him to his satisfaction.

"For the usual reasons." A man came through the door and jostled her, shoving her against Brian and cursing her for getting in his way.

Brian's arm came around her in a steel grip. "Back off," he snarled and, after a considering look, the man left them alone. "Come on," he said to Faith, his arm still holding her tight against his side.

She really, really wished it didn't feel so good to be near him.

Brian halted, unmoving, and stared at her, his gaze riveted to her chest. Her jacket had opened, and her brand-new pink blouse could be seen—ripped to expose her sheer white lacy bra. Her quick fix in the ladies' room obviously hadn't held. Hastily, she jerked the jacket closed again, but it was way too late.

His arm tightened and he uttered a brief, violent oath. "Where is the son of a bitch?"

Faith cursed herself for letting go of her jacket for even a moment. After the night she'd had, Brian going ballistic was the last thing she needed. "The bartender told you. The bouncer threw him out. Some time ago. So don't think you're going all macho on me and beating the hell out of him. I want to go home."

"He left you here. In this dive. After he—" He broke off and swore again, longer, harsher and even more explosively. "What did he do to you, Faith?"

"It's not as bad as it looks. Can we please go to your car? I'd really like to get out of here." She didn't know if he heard the quaver in her voice, but she knew it was there. "Please, Brian."

He didn't answer but walked her to the car. He'd brought his 'Vette and it looked as sleek and classy and out of place in the parking lot as its owner had inside the seedy bar. She huddled in her jacket, waiting for him to unlock the door, but instead he put his hands on her shoulders and turned her to face him.

He'd parked beneath the single light in the lot. His eyes were dark jade-green, serious and full of concern as he searched her face. His hands slid down her arms, then up again to cup her shoulders gently through the jacket. "Do I need to call the cops? Or take you to a hospital?"

"No." He didn't move and she added, "It wasn't anywhere near as bad as it looks. I swear."

"Will you tell me what happened?"

She would, but she was afraid she'd cry. And it was silly, really. Other than a ripped blouse she hadn't come to any harm. Nevertheless, she still felt like crying.

"I'll tell you, but only if you promise not to say I told you so."

His jaw tightened but his hands on her shoulders stayed gentle. "I wouldn't do that, Faith. Just tell me."

CHAPTER FOURTEEN

"TELL ME," Brian repeated. The bastard had ripped her shirt. He wanted to strangle the man for that alone. But what else had happened? Was a torn blouse the worst of it as she claimed, or had the man hurt her?

He gazed down at her and saw her lip tremble, her eyes fill with tears. His heart sank. "Damn. He did hurt you."

Tears slid down her cheeks in a slow trickle. She shook her head, tried to dash them away but then she started crying in earnest. He gathered her to his chest, put his hand on the back of her head and just held her. "Go ahead and cry, baby. It's okay. You just cry it out." He'd have time later to track the rat bastard down and make him pay.

Her hair smelled sweet and felt so soft, as soft as she did in his arms. He couldn't resist kissing the top of her head. Her arms had gone around his waist and her hands bunched in his shirt, holding on to it as if it were a lifeline. She said something against his chest, but the words were muffled by her sobs and from being pressed up against him. He continued to murmur reassurances until, finally, she lifted her head.

Her eyes were huge in her face, a deep chocolate-brown and wet with tears. His heart turned over and he wanted to hold her, protect her, forever.

Protect her? Forever? He'd never felt this way before. Not about anyone. Was it the circumstances…or was it Faith?

She raised her chin and a hard gleam came into her eyes. "I'm not hurt. I'm mad."

"Mad is good. Much better than hurt."

"He ripped my blouse—" she sniffed "—and it was b-b-brand-new."

"Faith, tell me the truth. Did he do anything more than rip your blouse?" If he had, they didn't need the police. Brian was going to kill the pervert himself.

"No. He would have. At least, I think he would have. But I stopped him."

"What did you do?"

"He followed me to the bathroom. He grabbed me from behind, and then turned me around. When I tried to get away, he grabbed me again and ripped my blouse. He tried to kiss me, which, obviously, I didn't want him to do. So I jabbed him in his carotid and then kneed him. Then I went to the bar and asked the bartender to have him thrown out."

She smiled. "Joe told Carlos—that's the bouncer, who's about seven feet tall—to take care of it. Which he did. Brent just went sailing through the air and landed in the dirt at the bottom of the stairs."

Though his lips twitched he was still too worried and far too angry, to be sidetracked. "Is that the whole story?"

She released him, stepped back and wrapped her arms around herself. "Most of it. I just want to get out of here, okay?"

His arms felt curiously empty without her in them. She wrapped her coat back around herself, covering up the ruined blouse. Which was a very good thing. After that first glance he'd tried his best not to look any lower than her face. He felt as slimy as the man who'd ripped her blouse in the first place, but he could hardly manage to tear his eyes away from the sight of those beautiful, full breasts barely concealed by the lacy bra. That wasn't the way he'd wanted to catch his first glimpse of Faith's lingerie.

Forget Faith's lingerie, he lectured himself. *And forget* first glimpse *because you're never getting a second one.*

"You were right," she said after they pulled away from the club. "Brent was a jerk and I should never have gone out with him."

Brian drove through the streets toward the highway. "He could just as easily have been a decent guy. You had bad luck, that's all." He wanted her to stay home and not date, but that wasn't fair to her. So he added, "Maybe next time you should try dating someone one of your friends knows." That way the guy wouldn't be a totally unknown quantity anyway.

"Another blind date?" She snorted derisively. "No thanks. Been there, done that. Maybe I should stay home and forget about dating for a while."

Sounded like a good plan to him. But again, he felt obliged to protest. "You're just upset about tonight. You'll change your mind."

"I'm not so sure about that," she said and lapsed into a silence that lasted until they reached the highway.

Her voice was low when she spoke again. "The night started out okay. The place he took me for dinner was all right. Not great, but not bad. But he kept trying to refill my wineglass and got really annoyed when I didn't want more than one glass. I finally got fed up with him and told him to take me home."

"Except he didn't." He concentrated on shifting in an attempt to curb his temper. Fourth…fifth…sixth. The 'Vette was smooth and driving was second nature, but it still gave him something else to focus on other than how much he wanted to get the guy alone for just five damn minutes.

"No, he went straight to the Rusty Nail. He wouldn't listen to anything I said. When we got there, he said he'd have just one drink and take me home, but by that point I didn't believe him. I just wanted to be rid of him."

Brian shot her a glance. She'd turned her head to look out the window, but he noticed her hand was clenched in a fist on her lap. He didn't speak, only waited for her to continue.

She shrugged. "You know the rest. One more lousy date."

"It was a little more than lousy, Faith. The man assaulted you. You should report him to the cops."

"Because he ripped my blouse? Come on, Brian. It's my word against his. He'd say it was an accident or deny doing it altogether."

It went against the grain to admit it but she was probably right. "No one else saw?"

"I don't think so. And I don't think I'd get a very credible witness anyway from a place like that."

They didn't speak for a while, and then shortly before they reached Aransas City, Faith broke the silence. "There's something else…. I know this is stupid but I can't help thinking about it."

"What? You said he didn't do anything else."

"He didn't. But tonight… It's my birthday. And I wanted to have fun and instead I ended up with the worst date ever. And a ripped blouse."

Why hadn't she told him her birthday was the day after Will's? "That's a pretty miserable birthday."

"I know," she said, and he thought he heard her sniffle.

A little while later they pulled into the driveway. "Faith, wait." He put a hand on her arm when she was about to get out. "Are you sure you're all right?"

"I'm sure." She looked into his eyes and smiled. "Thanks for coming to get me."

"Anytime you need me, I'll be there." He just hoped like hell she never needed him again for the same reason.

"I know." She leaned across and kissed his cheek. Her lips a light, gentle flutter on his skin, her scent subtle yet haunting. "Thank you, Brian," she said softly.

The next moment she was gone. Brian dropped his forehead down on the steering wheel. Oh, God, he was in deep trouble. She'd kissed his cheek—his cheek, for God's sake. And that innocent contact had touched him more than an entire night of hot, crazy sex with another woman ever had.

FAITH HAD A RESTLESS night, not entirely due to what had happened to her on the date.

The person who had disturbed her rest—again— was Brian. Why had she kissed him? Doing so had only increased the temptation to do more. She had no business kissing his cheek or any other part of him. But, oh, she wanted to. She wanted so badly to kiss him, really kiss him.

She thought about his mouth. How it hardened in anger. How it curved into that lady-killer smile. How it softened into tenderness when he looked at his son. What would it be like to feel those lips against hers? To have him hold her, put his hands on her? Make love to her.

She suspected she knew. Just as she knew that nothing like that could happen between them. Not only because she was his employee but because she and Brian didn't want the same things out of life.

Brian loved his son. He wanted to make a home for him and raise him. But he would never trust a woman with his heart. His childhood had seen to that. And she couldn't be with a man she knew could never fully commit to her.

Faith was not cut out for casual relationships. And Brian wasn't cut out for anything *but* that type of "relationship."

Faith wasn't ashamed of being traditional. That was who she was and she was comfortable with herself. She wanted love. She wanted marriage. She wanted a man who would love Lily and be a father to her.

Yet no matter how much Brian cared about her and Lily, no matter how much Faith cared about

Brian and Will, the four of them were not meant to be a family.

She knew it. Brian knew it, too.

CHAPTER FIFTEEN

"I STILL DON'T UNDERSTAND why we had to go Christmas shopping today," Faith said for about the third time since Brian had hustled her out the door Saturday afternoon. "We could have gone Tuesday during Mothers' Day Out and then Ava and Jack wouldn't have had to stay with the babies." She smiled. "Although, they really didn't seem to mind."

"Are you kidding? They couldn't wait to get their hands on those kids. You know they're trying to adopt, right?"

"No, I didn't. Oh, that's wonderful."

"Yeah. Ava said neither of them are looking forward to the empty nest when Cole goes off to college so they decided to adopt. And then when I mentioned babysitting, they jumped at the chance."

Brian congratulated himself on successfully diverting her. Not to mention, getting her out of the house in the first place. Faith had balked until he'd told her he really needed her help choosing the presents for all the kids in the family.

"It's still very nice of them. We shouldn't be too long, though, if you have your list ready. We're going to the discount store this time, right?"

Brian returned a noncommittal answer. He'd let her know he didn't mind shopping at the discount store for the kids' toys this time. Faith had been so bent out of shape over the prices in the other store after Will's birthday, he decided to humor her today. But where they ate dinner would be his choice. Not that Faith knew they were staying in Corpus Christi for dinner.

"Do you have *your* list ready?" he asked her. "You might as well get the gifts you need while we're out."

"I don't have many to get. I just have Will and Lily to buy for. And you."

He should tell her she didn't have to get him anything, but he didn't. He was curious about what she would buy for him. And he couldn't wait to see her reaction when she opened her birthday present. Earlier that morning he'd gone out and bought her what he always bought women. Jewelry. Brian had never known a woman who didn't like jewelry.

It wasn't a big deal, he rationalized. He'd given lots of women jewelry. Of course, he'd been dating them when he'd done it and he wasn't dating Faith. But he wanted to give her a gift and nothing else had occurred to him. He'd asked the store to deliver it to the yacht that he'd reserved for a dinner cruise. It should be waiting for her when they boarded.

He couldn't make Faith forget what a terrible birthday she'd had, but he could at least show her a good time tonight. Which was why he'd arranged for a private dinner cruise on *The Crystal Ship*. He'd called first thing that morning and had to sweet-talk—and when that didn't work, bribe—them into taking his reservation on such short notice. He'd wanted to take her someplace special and he'd heard good things about this dinner cruise.

But it wasn't a date. He was simply being a friend, trying to make up for how bad the night before had been for her. If it had been a date, he could think about kissing Faith. Touching her. Making love to her. But it wasn't a date, so he wouldn't think about kissing her. Touching her. Making love to her.

"Brian, you missed the exit."

"Sorry. I'll take the next one." *Pay attention to your driving and quit fantasizing about Faith*, he told himself. Fantasizing was dangerous in more ways than one.

"What time is your date tonight?"

"My date?" he repeated blankly.

"Yes, your date with the incredibly beautiful former model. Marissa, wasn't it? Surely you haven't forgotten."

Oh, shit. "Oh, that. Yeah, she broke it. And her name's Virginia." Corinna was not going to be happy with him, but she'd get over it.

"Why?"

He parked and shot her an annoyed glance. "How do I know? She said she had to wash her hair."

Faith stared at him. "You're kidding. Did she really say that?"

"I don't know." He shrugged. "I wasn't paying attention. She went into some long explanation but I stopped listening after I heard 'break the date.'"

"That doesn't bother you? That she not only canceled on you but gave you such an obviously lame excuse?" she asked curiously.

"No." He picked up his cell phone from the compartment in the dash and slipped it into his pocket. "It was just a date. Not a big deal."

"You acted like it was the other night."

"Are you going to get out of the car or are we going to sit here all day while you give me the third degree about a woman I've already forgotten?"

"Don't be grumpy at me. *I* didn't break the date."

God, how did he get himself into these things? He pinched the bridge of his nose. Why was nothing ever simple with Faith? "Sorry."

He handed her his list of names that went on for half a mile. How in the hell did he end up with such a big family? "Why don't you go on in and I'll meet you in the toy department. I have to make a phone call. To a client," he added.

"All right." She gave him a puzzled look, but she got out and walked across the parking lot.

He'd never watched Faith walk before. She walked very…gracefully. She was wearing jeans. Not too tight. As if there were such a thing. But Faith's jeans were just tight enough to look really, really fine on her. He stared after her for a minute before he remembered the call he needed to make.

Fortunately, he reached Corinna's answering machine. "Hey, it's Brian. I have to cancel tonight. Something came up with work. Sorry. I'll, uh, call you." He intentionally didn't say *when* he'd call her.

He snapped the phone closed. Something told him that he'd seen the last of Corinna. He'd not only broken their date; he'd left the message on the machine. Oh, well. Easy come, easy go.

It worried him a little that he'd rather be with a woman he knew he couldn't take to bed than the hot number he knew he could. But then he shook it off. He was doing something nice for his son's nanny. No big deal. Nothing to worry about.

Right.

BRIAN WAS ACTING strangely. He was up to something, she was sure of it. What, she didn't know.

But I mean, really, Faith thought. What was all that about the broken date with Ms. Lingerie Model? That was bizarre in itself. And now they'd gone through his shopping list and taken care of nearly everyone on it. Except one last present he'd been dragging his feet about.

"You know, Max is five, Brian. He won't care if you give him the ultimate toy or not. He'll like whatever you get him." And if what she'd seen and heard about the adorable little boy was any indication, he'd probably break it within the day. Brian had considered and rejected a remote control car for that very reason.

Brian checked his watch. Something else he'd been doing often. "All right, all right." He reached for a toy. The very one she'd suggested he get for Max in the first place. Twenty minutes and seventy-five toys ago.

"So, you think he'll like this one?"

She barely swallowed a shriek. "Yes, Brian," she said, trying not to grit her teeth. "I think you should buy him that one."

"You sound a little grumpy."

She gave him a dirty look but didn't answer directly. "It's getting late. It will be dinnertime before too long. Shouldn't we get home?"

He stacked the last item precariously on top of the pile in the cart and began pushing it toward the

checkout, while she followed with her own cart.
Given the number of children they were buying for,
they'd needed two carts.

"I think we should have dinner in Corpus. I mentioned to Ava that depending on when we finished
the shopping, we might do that and she said they'd
get a pizza delivered or something."

"But Ava and Jack have already been there all afternoon. And if we stay out much later then they'll
have to bathe the children and put them to bed."

"I think two adults should be able to handle
bedtime for Will and Lily. Besides, it will give them
some practice for when they have their own baby.
I know I would have appreciated some of that."

She wavered. "I don't know. I haven't left Lily this
long since I worked full-time at the leasing office."

"If you want to check on the kids, give Ava a call."

"Okay." She pulled out her cell and dialed the
house. Ava answered and assured her the kids were
fine and that she and Jack were happy to stay as long
as they needed them.

"And I want to hear all about dinner," Ava added.

"What?" They'd reached the front of the line and
the clerk was ringing up all their purchases. "Wait,
those are mine." She retrieved a couple of the items
that she wanted to buy for Will and Lily and set
them aside to pay for separately. "I've got to go,
Ava, before your brother pulls one over on me."

"Okay, have fun. Don't worry about the kids, we're loving staying with them."

She hung up and grabbed several other items that were hers. With only two children to buy for, she had splurged a little. She could afford it and it was Lily's first Christmas and Will's first with his dad, after all.

"I could have gotten those," Brian said.

"No, you couldn't. These are my gifts to the children. You don't need to pay for my presents."

"It's a few toys, Faith."

"Which I'm paying for." He shrugged but he didn't argue anymore. "Brian, why did Ava say she wanted to hear all about dinner? Did you plan to have dinner out before we left?" And if he had, why hadn't he told her?

"You must have heard wrong," he said, and handed the clerk his credit card.

She didn't think so, but she let it drop. She paid for her purchases and they took the carts to the car and stuffed all the sacks of toys inside. "Wow, that was an experience," she said as she buckled her seat belt. "I wonder what it's like on Christmas Eve?"

"I don't know, but I don't plan to find out. How does seafood sound?"

"I love seafood. And I'm starving."

"Good. I know just the place."

Faith didn't pay attention to where he was going

until they reached the harbor. "We can't go any place fancy, you know. I'm wearing jeans." Besides, she knew he wouldn't let her pay for dinner and she didn't want him to have to buy her an expensive meal. Not that Brian cared, but it didn't seem right.

"You look fine. Don't worry, we can go to this place just like we are."

Maybe he could. He was wearing nice khakis and a long-sleeve, baby-blue, button-down shirt. He looked perfect, as usual. She didn't, as usual. She could put on some lipstick, at least. She rummaged around in her purse, found her hairbrush and brushed her hair. When he stopped, she pulled down the visor to look in the mirror and apply her lipstick. There, it would have to do. She pressed her lips together, added a dab more lipstick and turned to find Brian staring at her.

"What?" She glanced back in the mirror but didn't see any problems.

He cleared his throat. "You don't usually wear lipstick. I've never seen you…put it on."

She stuffed the lipstick and brush back in her purse. "I don't ever wear it at home. Just if I go out."

Brian got out and came around to open her door. For the first time, Faith noticed where they were. In the harbor marina by the big boats. "Where's the restaurant?" Puzzled, she looked around, but she didn't see a likely looking building.

"We're having dinner on that boat right over there." He motioned to a yacht named *The Crystal Ship*.

He took her arm to walk with her, but she stopped and stared at him with her mouth open. "That's a yacht, not a boat."

"Whatever." He started walking again, moving her along with him. "It's a dinner cruise. Goes up and down the canals and along the Laguna Madre."

"You booked a dinner cruise? When? Why?"

"This morning." He stopped at the gangplank leading to the yacht and smiled at her. Her heart fluttered. "I wanted to surprise you."

"You succeeded." Surprise? Stunned was more like it. "Brian, I can't—we can't eat here. On this— this yacht." Go on a cruise, a romantic cruise with Brian? It was such a thoughtful gesture. But she couldn't possibly accept. Could she? Oh, what was he doing to her poor, silly heart?

"Sure we can." He caught her hands and held them. "I know it's not your birthday, but I thought since you had such a crappy time on your actual birthday that maybe we could do something fun tonight."

Something fun? She'd never done anything like this in her life. Oh, she'd had dates take her nice places. And Lily's father had occasionally taken her to a fancy restaurant, but nothing like this.

"I thought you said you were starving?"

She'd just had a taste of that legendary smooth

charm of his. And fool that she was, she was falling for it just as hard as she imagined all those other women had. All those women he'd dated and dropped.

"Faith, it's just dinner. Not a seduction." His voice was deep and amused.

She flushed. Of course he wouldn't seduce her. She wasn't his type and she knew that as well as he did. Just because he might be a little attracted to her didn't mean he wanted…anything. It didn't mean he intended to do…anything. She sucked in a breath, her stomach fluttering.

"You shouldn't have gone to so much trouble. But thank you."

He was still holding her hands.

Undoubtedly, she was making a huge mistake. But she simply didn't have it in her to stop herself. He kept one of her hands in his as they walked up the gangplank and stepped inside another world. Elegance. Beauty. Romance.

He smiled at her, that wicked, sexy smile she loved so much.

Oh, Faith. You're toast.

CHAPTER SIXTEEN

"Am I going to turn into a pumpkin at midnight?"
Faith asked Brian.

Brian laughed. "The coach turned into a pumpkin. Not Cinderella. And you don't have an evil
stepmother so you couldn't possibly be Cinderella
anyway." He tapped his wineglass against hers.
"Happy birthday, Faith."

"Thank you. I'm…a little overwhelmed. No
one's ever done anything like this for me before."

Which was a crime. She deserved a man who
would make her feel special. Not a man who'd
desert her when she needed him, as Lily's father
had. And not a man like him, either, he acknowl-
edged. A man who couldn't give her the happy
ending she should have.

She sipped her wine and looked out over the
water, then glanced at him, her lips curving upward.
"Did you arrange for the spectacular sunset, too?"

He returned the smile. "No, that was just luck."
Faith was right, the sunset was gorgeous. Pinks

merged into shimmering red against the backdrop of the deep indigo ocean and the darkening blue of the sky. But beautiful as it was, the sunset didn't hold a candle to Faith.

Her eyes sparkled with pleasure; her cheeks were pink with the chill of the wind on the water. Her face radiated happiness.

Oh, God, what in the hell was wrong with him? He'd just compared a woman to a sunset. "Are you cold? If you are, we can go inside and sit by the window."

"Not yet. It's so beautiful out here. I want to watch the sun set from the deck."

But the thin jacket she wore wasn't much protection from the chill. He took off his leather jacket and put it around her shoulders. Tempted to let his hands linger, instead he let go and stuck them in his pockets.

"But won't you be cold?"

"Nah, I'm tough."

She laughed and put up a hand to his coat, stroking the leather. "What kind of leather is this? I've never felt anything so soft."

"Beats me. I walked into a store in Italy, said, 'That looks good,' and bought it."

"Italian leather. No wonder it feels so incredible." She sighed. "Don't you ever shop for bargains?"

"Honey, I don't shop at all if I can help it."

She chuckled. "Spoken like a true man. My dad

didn't like to shop, either, but when he did, he never paid what they asked. For anything. He was a champion haggler. And my mom could pinch a penny tighter than anyone I ever knew."

"Is that why you're so thrifty?"

"Maybe. Plus, I've had to be."

"Because of Lily." Because the son of a bitch who'd gotten her pregnant had run out on her.

"Yes." She sighed. "I wish my parents had lived to see Lily. They'd have loved her so much."

"When did they pass away?"

"Five years ago. They'd always wanted to go to Europe and had saved until they were finally able to swing it. They did one of those tours of twelve countries in ten days, or something like that. But they never came back. Their train crashed in the mountains in Switzerland."

"I'm sorry. You obviously still miss them." He could hear the love for them in her voice.

"Always will. But I was lucky. They were terrific parents. I had a good foundation and now I have something to strive for with my own daughter."

"You're a good mother, Faith." He raised his hand and touched the backs of his fingers to her cheek. It was soft, as soft as her baby's skin. "You're frozen. Let's go inside. I think they're ready to feed us."

He took her hand and led her into the cabin. The lights were low, the furnishings elegant. The table was set with a pure white tablecloth, sparkling crystal, gleaming silverware, candles flickering romantically. A silver bowl filled with camellias floating on water stood as a centerpiece.

He immediately recognized the muted strains of classical music that played in the background. The Romeros playing Vivaldi guitar concertos was one of his favorite CDs. He had to admit *The Crystal Ship* did a nice job, and he was critical, having dined in some spectacular and expensive restaurants over the years and in many parts of the world.

He pulled out her chair and then took his own seat. The waiter discreetly appeared, offering them more wine and the first course. They'd had appetizers out on the deck, tiny canapes of crab and shrimp, served by the same man. "I'll wait until the main course."

"I should wait, too," Faith said. "One is usually my limit. If Will or Lily wakes up—"

"I'll take care of them," Brian said. "You can have another glass."

"You don't have to do that."

"I want to."

Her eyes softened. "Thank you," she said huskily.

She let the waiter fill her glass and started on the salad of field greens, pecans and apples with crumbled bits of blue cheese. "This is wonderful." She took another bite and chewed slowly. He leaned back in his chair and smiled, enjoying her obvious pleasure in the food.

She glanced around the room. "I'm sure this was terribly expensive. You really shouldn't have done it."

"I'm enjoying myself, too, you know. Relax, Faith." He didn't think he'd ever had a date with a woman who worried so much about him spending money on her. Given the chance, most of them went through it like water. But then, he'd never troubled to look for a woman who wasn't that way.

Once they were served their main course, a pan-seared red snapper in a creamy, delicate wine sauce, Faith took a bite and sighed. "Up to now, tournedos was always my favorite, but this is amazing." She ate for a moment before looking at him with pure delight.

"I have a confession to make. I've never been on a cruise before. Actually, I've never even been on a boat ride before. This is a first for me."

He'd never been with a woman who embraced life with her exuberance. Never known a woman who was willing to share even little pleasures with him and expect nothing in return.

The women he dated were beautiful, jaded, accustomed to being showered with gifts and the trappings of wealth. They would never dream of openly showing such joy in a new experience, as Faith had, and sharing that with him.

Those women were shallow, and he had never

minded that in the past. Faith was anything but shallow. She was open and honest and loving. He'd seen her get as much enjoyment from eating pizza, playing with the babies or watching a movie at home as she appeared to be taking from this cruise.

"It's a first for me, too."

She sent him a doubtful look and took a sip of wine. "I don't believe you. You've been all over the world and you're telling me you've never been on a boat?"

"I've been on plenty of boats. Cruise ships, ski boats, fishing boats. But I've never been on a sunset cruise with a woman I consider a friend." He took a bite of snapper. "To tell you the honest truth, I've never been friends with a woman before. Not one who isn't related to me in some way."

"You don't think of any of the women you've dated as friends?"

He laughed shortly. "No, friendship has never been what they wanted from me." They wanted to be wined and dined and gifted with presents. And they wanted sex. But friendship? Never. He ate some more snapper and mulled that over.

"You're not interested in friendship, either, are you? Not with women."

"I never have been in the past."

"But now you've changed your mind?"

"I don't know. I do know I like being friends with

you. But other women—" He lifted his shoulder in a shrug. Strangely enough, even though he fantasized about taking Faith to bed, he did think of her as a friend. He'd never experienced that before.

Finished, he laid down his fork. "My life has changed a lot since I found out about Will." And since he'd met Faith. She had changed his mind about a lot of things.

"I know what you mean. Children have a huge impact on our lives, don't they?" Faith put down her fork and leaned back. "I can't eat another bite."

"Don't forget about dessert. The waiter said something about white chocolate bread pudding. Here he comes now," he added. The man placed the fragrant desserts in front of them and vanished.

Faith moaned. "You're evil." She looked at her dish. "What woman could resist this?"

But she didn't pick up her spoon. "What are you waiting for? Dig in."

"If you must know, I'm reminding myself how tight my jeans were this morning and trying to talk myself out of eating it. But it's not working."

He smiled. "Trust me on this, Faith. Your jeans are nowhere near too tight."

She shot him a thoughtful glance. "I suppose a few bites won't hurt. It would be rude not to taste it."

"True. Besides, it's your birthday. I've heard calories don't count on your birthday."

"That's right. Just like whatever you eat when you're standing up has no calories." She paused before eating and said, "Maybe I should stand, to be safe."

They both laughed. He watched her eat it slowly, savoring every bite. Resolutely, she laid down her spoon after she'd eaten about a quarter of it. "Aren't you going to eat yours? It's delicious."

"I was having fun watching you. You missed a crumb, though. Right here." He wiped his finger over the corner of her mouth, then licked it. "Yum."

She laughed. "You couldn't possibly taste it from that tiny bit. Here, try mine." She scooped some onto her spoon and held it out to him.

He opened his mouth and waited for her to feed it to him. After a brief hesitation, she slipped the spoon inside. He ate it and ran his tongue over his lips before wiping his napkin over them.

"It's good. Not as sweet as I'd like it, though. I have a real weakness for sweets. Desserts, candy." He paused and met her gaze. "Women."

Her eyes widened. A deep, rich chocolate-brown that whet a man's appetite.

"Women aren't sweets," she said huskily.

"No, but you are. Sweet. Very sweet."

Her eyes widened even more. She touched her tongue to her lips, unconsciously, he was sure. He wondered if it were possible to die from wanting to kiss a woman this badly.

Not just any woman. He wanted to kiss Faith.

"I— I need to—" She rose, obviously flustered. "I'll be back."

She walked out of the room quickly. In fact, she very nearly ran.

He signaled the waiter and asked him to bring the present that had been delivered earlier that day. Something told him Faith wasn't going to respond to the gift as most of the women he knew would. He was anxious to see her reaction.

What the hell are you doing? he asked himself. Wining her, dining her, romancing her. Fantasizing about kissing her, making love to her.

Oh, God. He was falling for Faith.

IN THE RESTROOM, Faith put her hands to her cheeks and willed her heart rate to slow down. She was not successful. Brian was making her crazy.

He wanted her. He wanted to kiss her, to take her to bed. She wasn't a total idiot. She could tell when a man was flirting with her. When a man wanted her.

Yes, you are an idiot, her sane self argued. Brian wanted her *for now.* But once he'd had her, the thrill would be gone. It wouldn't last. Couldn't possibly last. Faith would be heartbroken and he would move on. To other more beautiful, more sophisticated women. To women who were his type. To women without babies and complications. To women who were players, just as he was.

What if he just needs the right woman? the starry-eyed idealist side of her argued.

Oh, and you're that woman, I suppose? Ms. Sane scoffed. *Get real, Faith.*

She didn't want to get real. Didn't want to be practical, as she'd been her entire life. Especially since Lily had been born.

I'm celebrating my birthday. I'm on a dinner cruise. Why shouldn't I be with a charming man?

Why shouldn't she enjoy him? Even…kiss him. Kissing would be all right, wouldn't it? She couldn't go to bed with him, not without risking too much. Such as her foolish heart. But surely she could kiss him without taking too great a risk. Couldn't she?

She needed to pull herself together. She refused to hide in the bathroom for the remainder of the most romantic, magical night of her life. For once she would simply enjoy herself and leave all the analyzing and worrying to the sane side of her, who could deal with it in the morning.

Tonight, she decided, she would leave Ms. Sane in the bathroom.

CHAPTER SEVENTEEN

SHE FOUND HIM standing by the window, looking out at the lights twinkling along the shore. When he turned and smiled as she entered the room, Faith felt the urge to run a finger, then her mouth, over the sexy curve of his lips. She wanted to put her arms around his neck and kiss him, press her body up against him and feel the hardness and strength of him.

"I thought you might have jumped ship," he said, amusement in his voice.

"Now why would I do that?" She walked over to him and gave him what she hoped was a sultry smile.

He grinned but didn't answer. Instead he pulled from his pocket a long, slim, black velvet box tied up with a silver ribbon. "And that would have been a shame since I haven't given you your present yet." He held it out to her. "Happy birthday, Faith."

She whipped her hands behind her back. "You've already given me this cruise. I don't need another present."

He reached for her and gently coaxed one of

her hands, then placed the box in it. "Yes, you do. Everyone needs a present to open on their birthday."

It appeared to be a box that jewelry would come in. A bracelet or a necklace. Surely he hadn't given her jewelry.

She looked at the gift again, then at him. The corner of his mouth lifted into a beguiling smile as she stared at him. Smooth. Charming.

What was she thinking? This was Brian Kincaid. Of course he'd bought her jewelry.

She tugged at the end of the ribbon and let it fall, hesitating before she opened the box. Her breath caught in her throat. A slim, delicate bracelet of white gold and blue topaz sparkled against a background of black velvet. It was the most beautiful thing she'd ever seen. She shut the box with a snap, afraid if she looked at it for too long she would never refuse it.

"I can't accept this."

"Now why am I not surprised you said that," he murmured, taking the box from her and opening it. He took out the bracelet and dangled it from his fingers. "Let's see what it looks like on. Don't you like it?"

"Of course I like it. It's gorgeous. I'd have to be crazy not to like it." She stood, still in shock, as he clasped it around her wrist.

"There. Fits perfectly."

"That's not the point." She sucked in her breath, attempting to be resolute. "You can't buy me jewelry. It's too expensive. It's too…" Her voice trailed off. Intimate. She imagined he bought all his women jewelry. All of his lovers. Which she wasn't.

Oh, but she wanted to be.

"Brian, you're incredibly kind to give me something this beautiful, but I really can't accept it. I work for you. It wouldn't be right."

He laughed. "Why are you making such a big deal out of a little present?"

"It's not a little present. A little present is a book or a CD. Not an absolutely stunning bracelet." She looked at her wrist again. It suited her, she realized. Something she would have picked herself if she'd ever shopped for such a thing. The sky-blue stones sparkled in the candlelight. She wanted to keep the bracelet so badly she needed all her strength to resist.

"You shouldn't buy me jewelry. I work for you," she repeated.

"Not tonight, you don't." He took her hand in his and with his other one, lightly ran a finger underneath the slim band. He gazed into her eyes and she felt as if she were drowning in the brilliant green of his. "Tonight we're just Brian and Faith. I want you to keep the bracelet, Faith. It would make me very happy if you would."

Gorgeous pools of jade. Dark green and fringed with long black lashes. Utterly bewitching. "You're tempting me." With the bracelet…and so much more.

"I hope so." He moved closer to her and his voice lowered. "Because you've been tempting me for weeks now."

How was she to respond to that? Especially since she'd left her sanity in the bathroom. "We shouldn't go there."

"Why not?" He lifted her wrist to his lips and kissed it, just below where the bracelet lay.

Her skin tingled with the contact. Why not? A million reasons. And the most crucial was because she was falling in love with him.

Brian slid his arm around her waist and took her other hand in his, holding it against his chest. "Dance with me, Faith," he murmured in her ear.

How could she not? She closed her eyes and let herself relax, let herself move with him. He danced well, which didn't surprise her. She found she did, too, when she danced with him.

"Are you going to keep the bracelet?"

"I don't know. I shouldn't." She sighed and leaned her cheek against his chest. "But you're very persuasive." Which he undoubtedly knew. So she decided to have a little fun with him.

She owed him one for flustering her so badly, "Did you know the blue topaz is my birthstone?"

"The saleslady told me. That's why I chose that particular bracelet."

"Do you know what it means? What the stone stands for?"

Puzzled, he looked down at her. "It's supposed to stand for something?"

"Oh, yes." She nodded solemnly. "All gemstones do. They all have a meaning."

"What kind of meaning?"

"For instance, the birth stone for March is the aquamarine," she said in her best lecturer's voice. "It symbolizes youth and hope." She kept her eyes on his when she told him, "The blue topaz stands for love. And fidelity," she added, twisting the knife. She let that sink in then added, "Still want me to keep it?"

He actually paled. God love him, just as she thought, he hadn't had a clue. She laughed out loud. "If you could only see your face right now. It's priceless." She patted his cheek. "Gotcha."

His eyes narrowed. "Now who's the evil one? A blue topaz doesn't mean love and fidelity?"

"No, it does. But you clearly had no idea what you were doing, so you're off the hook."

He didn't speak, but gathered her close once again as the song faded into another. James Blunt's evocative voice. She'd heard the song, of course. But she'd never *felt* the song. Never felt…beautiful. Not like she did in Brian's arms. *You're beautiful, it's true…*

"Faith."

She looked up into those sensual green eyes.

"You are, you know."

She stared at him, mesmerized.

"You're beautiful," he said. Just before he kissed her.

Faith closed her eyes and put her arms around his neck, indulging herself in his kiss. In the feather-light touch of his lips against hers, his tongue slipping into her mouth, gently teasing, seeking an answer. She responded with her own tongue, tasting him. Dark, potent, masculine. And very, very know-ledgeable.

Slowly, he ended the kiss, with one last meeting of their lips. He still held her in his arms. The music played on. But her world had changed. She'd never shared a more perfect kiss.

He shook his head and said, "Damn," so softly she barely heard him. Then he bent his head and kissed her again. His arms tightened around her and she melted into him. One of his hands slid up her back and into her hair, angling her head so he could kiss her more fully.

Her knees turned to putty even as her breasts tightened, tingling with anticipation. But he didn't touch her breasts, didn't push her. He simply kissed her, consumed her, softly at first, then hotter and deeper and wilder, before he finally drew back.

If she hadn't known better she'd have said he looked bemused. But that was crazy. Brian Kincaid, bemused by a couple of kisses? Not possible.

"Faith."

"What?" She felt breathless. He'd driven all the air from her lungs. With a kiss. What would making love with him do to her?

"We're back at the dock. We need to go." He released her and she stood there for a moment, feeling adrift.

If the cruise hadn't ended when it did… If he'd wanted to she knew he could have taken off her clothes on the spot. Or she'd have taken them off for him. She'd have stepped willingly back into his arms. Into his bed.

And if he asked her when they reached home… she still might.

NEITHER OF THEM spoke much on the way home. Brian didn't know what Faith was thinking but he knew he'd lost his mind enough for both of them.

Who'd have guessed Faith would come alive like that in his arms? He could still feel her soft curves. Taste her, as sweet as he'd imagined, but sexy, even a little exotic.

Brian had kissed a lot of women. Some good. Some very, very good. Some bad, some mediocre. But he'd never been completely turned inside out by a simple kiss. Two kisses. Until he'd kissed Faith tonight.

Naturally, instead of putting distance between them as he should, he was holding her hand. Had been holding it since they'd walked off the boat.

What did that say about him? That he was completely nuts, that's what.

He could have her in his bed tonight. He knew it as well as he knew his own name. He could touch her breasts, cup them in his hands, suckle them. He could caress her rear, pressing her against him, feeling every blessed curve against his own naked body. Taste every inch of her and slide inside her and make love to her until—

"What are you thinking?"

"Uh…nothing." *Brilliant response, Brian.*

"Are you sure? You're squeezing my hand really hard. I thought you might be upset."

He immediately loosened his hold on her poor hand, though he kept it in his. Damn, what a moron he was. "Sorry, I didn't realize I was doing that." He glanced at her but he couldn't read her expression in the dark. "I'm not upset. Why would I be?" Crazy, maybe. But not upset.

"I don't know." She was quiet a moment, then said, "I had a wonderful time tonight. The cruise and… everything was amazing. I wish it didn't have to end."

This was where he could tell her it didn't have

to end. That they could take it to the bedroom and make each other very happy. But he didn't say it.

If they made love, Faith would regret it. And so would he. Getting involved with Faith, taking her to bed, was a mistake. He knew it. She knew it, too.

A short time later they pulled up to the house. Once Jack and Ava left and they had checked on both soundly sleeping babies, they went back into the living room.

"Do you want a nightcap?"

Faith shook her head, smiling faintly. "Thanks, but I had plenty on the boat. But you go ahead."

He didn't want a drink. He wanted Faith. "I'll pass on it, too."

"I'm not sure how to thank you for everything you did for me tonight. It was…magic."

He smiled. "For me, too."

"Really?"

"It surprises you that tonight was special for me?" She didn't answer, just looked at him with those beautiful brown eyes. "Tonight has meant a lot to me…but not as much as you do." He was turning into a sap but she seemed to have that effect on him. He put his hand on her arm. "Faith, the night doesn't have to end now."

For a long moment she said nothing. "If it doesn't, you know what will happen."

"I know. I want to make love to you, Faith. And I think you want the same thing."

Her eyes were an even darker brown now, brimming with emotion. Sadness? "Sometimes… Sometimes I want what—who—I can't have. I don't think I can have you, Brian. I'm nearly certain I can't."

"But you're not sure, are you?"

"No, and I don't think you are, either." She put her hand around his neck, then guided his head down until she could reach him. As she'd done the night before, she laid her lips lightly, gently against his cheek. "Next time you ask me, if you ask me again, you need to be sure. Because I won't have the strength to say no again."

He knew he should be glad she'd saved them both from making a disastrous mistake. But, damn it all, he wasn't.

CHAPTER EIGHTEEN

"THIS IS THE BIGGEST Christmas tree I've ever had," Faith said the weekend after her birthday. "I didn't think it would fit in the living room."

"I told you it would. Hand me that angel and I'll put it on the top." Brian hadn't decorated a Christmas tree in years. Not since he was a kid and Mark had forced him and Jay into shopping for one. Once they'd brought it home Mark had done the lion's share of the work. He smiled, remembering the mess he and Jay had made of the strands of lights and, worse, the tinsel icicles they'd started a fight with. For the next month, Mark grumbled whenever he found another strand of the stringy silver stuff. Their oldest brother had yelled a lot, but Brian and Jay had always known he was a soft touch.

Though Faith had put on some Christmas music, both the babies were shrieking so loudly in their playpens, it couldn't really be heard. "Sounds like Will and Lily are ready to be sprung," he said, climbing down the ladder.

Faith stared at the tree critically, her head angled. "All right, but I think it's lopsided. Come see what you think. If you look at it from where I'm standing, it seems to be leaning in the other direction."

He didn't look because he didn't intend to do anything about it even if the damn tree was at forty-five degrees. He lifted Lily out and put her down on the carpet. She immediately headed to her mother. She'd started crawling about three weeks before and she'd taken off in no time. Will, naturally, homed in on the tree, with Brian behind him.

"The tree is perfectly straight." It had better be, since Faith had made him mess around with the thing for half an hour before she was satisfied and they could even begin to decorate. He stepped on a stray ornament and winced when he heard a crunch. "Who knew you were such a perfectionist?" He bent down to pick up the pieces and throw them away.

She frowned at him. "I'm not being a perfectionist. I simply want to make sure the tree is sturdy so it doesn't fall over on one of the kids." She handed Lily the pink hippo, her favorite toy since the moment she'd set eyes on it. The baby gave a little chortle of laughter and hugged the hippo.

"It won't fall over, Faith." She was bent over, adjusting something at the bottom of the tree. She had on the same jeans she'd worn the night he'd taken her to dinner. He couldn't help admiring the way she filled them out... Grimly, he tried to steer his thoughts in another direction. Any other direction. He'd had a hell of a time keeping his hands to himself since he'd kissed her, but he'd done it. He just wasn't sure how much longer he could resist the urge to touch her, to run his hands over every inch of that soft, curvy body. To hold her and kiss her—

Damn it, he was doing it again.

"What time did you want to take the babies to get their pictures taken with Santa tomorrow?"

He'd forgotten about that. The mall. Santa. A million screaming, crying children. And he'd said he'd go. He must have been nuts. Still, this was Lily's and Will's first Christmas. He'd feel like Scrooge if he didn't get their pictures done, and he knew Faith needed his help.

"Second thoughts?" Faith asked, as if reading his mind.

"No. I said I'd do it and I will. Might as well go first thing. I'll head out to work after we get back."

"It might not be as bad as you think."

"You just keep telling yourself that," he said and she laughed.

Will was busy trying to pull the ornaments off the bottom branches of the tree. Which was why they hadn't hung anything fragile down low. "Maybe we should have skipped the lower branches entirely," he said as Will managed to yank one of the three wise men off and stuff the soft ornament in his mouth.

"Here you go, son." He exchanged the wise man for a toy train, which held the kid's attention for all of twenty seconds.

Will abandoned the train and crawled over to the coffee table and his favorite toy, the wooden spoon. He pulled himself up to stand and banged the spoon on the table as hard as he could. Making noise was something he never tired of doing.

Brian sat in the easy chair and reflected that at this rate he'd need a new coffee table in about a month.

"You really shouldn't let him beat on the coffee table like that."

They'd had this argument before, but arguing was better than thinking about kissing her. "Why? He likes it and it keeps him occupied."

"Because he'll do it at your brothers' and sister's houses and they might not want him to ruin their coffee tables. Oddly enough, some people like their furniture and don't want it destroyed."

He waved her objection aside. "They all have kids. You can't tell me Max hasn't demolished any number of things in his lifetime. The kid's a hellion. I'm not sure Miranda is much better. And don't even get me started on Jason. He's just like his father. Jay never saw a toy he didn't want to take apart."

Faith sat on the floor with Lily in her lap. "Are you sure *Jay* took them apart? Something tells me you would have been the instigator there."

He had to smile at that. "He didn't need much encouragement, believe me. I liked to rebuild things after he took them apart. Electronics, mostly. I tried to put in a surround sound system when I was about fifteen. Mark was not happy with all the holes I put in the ceiling. Not to mention, I managed to blow the TV when I turned it on."

"Dada, Dada, Dada," Will chanted. He let go of the table and stepped toward Brian.

"Look, he took a step. He's trying to walk again." Will had been on the verge of walking for some time, but tonight was the first time Brian had seen him take a completely unassisted step.

Brian held out his hands. "That's it, come on, Will. Come to Daddy."

Will had screwed up his mouth and furrowed his brow in concentration. Wavering for a moment, he gathered himself and took two more staggering steps before tumbling into Brian's arms and laughing madly.

"Attaboy! You did it! You did it!" Brian scooped him up and kissed his cheek while Will's chubby arm went around his neck.

"Dada."

"That's right. Daddy." His eyes met Faith's

across the room. He wanted to say something but found he couldn't speak.

Faith wiped at her eyes, her mouth curved into a gentle smile.

"He took his first steps," Brian finally managed to say. "Can you beat that?"

When Will had first come into his life, he'd had no idea he would feel this incredible rush of love for his son. No idea he'd even be capable of feeling such an emotion so strongly. He'd spent his entire adult life carefully avoiding entanglements for this very reason.

Will squirmed in Brian's arms, anxious to explore again. Brian set him down on the carpet and he started crawling toward Faith, who lovingly watched him with Lily in her lap.

"Mama. Mama," Lily chanted.

"Mama, Mama," his son echoed, as he reached Faith's side and demanded to be picked up.

"Faith. I'm Faith, Will."

"Mama," he insisted, patting her.

Faith didn't look at Brian, but she scooped Will into her lap and gathered him close, cuddling him as she did Lily. "I've been trying to teach him to call me Faith. But Lily has started calling me Mama and he hears her and then he…" Her voice trailed off and she still wouldn't look at him.

"It's natural, I guess. That's not the first time, is it?"

But it was the first time Brian had heard him say it to Faith and without screaming for his dead mother.

She shook her head, finally facing him. "He's been saying 'Mama,' of course, but a few days ago he actually said it to me. I don't want you to think I've encouraged him. But he gets confused…" She kissed Will's cheek, then Lily's. "I don't know what to do about it."

"Faith, it's not a big deal. Don't stress about it." Except it was a big deal. A very big, damn scary deal.

A FEW NIGHTS LATER, Brian came into the kitchen, where Faith was feeding the babies dinner. He didn't say anything at first, just stood there watching her and the children.

"Is something wrong?" she finally asked. "I heard the phone ring but I couldn't get it."

"No, nothing's wrong. It was for me." He put his hands in his pockets and leaned against the counter. "Can you keep Will for me on Friday night?"

Faith looked up from feeding Lily. "Of course. Are you doing some more Christmas shopping?" Lily grabbed the spoon Faith held and tried to steer it to her mouth, but instead launched the carrots at her mother, where they landed in a nice, big orange glob on Faith's favorite white sweater. She looked down in dismay. Served her right. What kind of idiot fed a baby while wearing white?

She glanced at Brian, who still hadn't answered her. He looked uncomfortable, she realized. Even… guilty. Now why would he look guilty?

"Not shopping. I have a date. For a…a Christmas party."

Her heart sank. A date. He hadn't been out with another woman since before her birthday. The dinner cruise, that magical, wonderful night she couldn't stop thinking about. Couldn't stop reliving. Couldn't stop imagining a different ending for—if she'd followed her heart instead of her head.

Poor, silly Faith, wanting a man, a family, she couldn't have.

Brian had no reason to feel guilty. There were no commitments between them. They hadn't made love, hadn't done anything beyond share a couple of kisses. Kisses that had meant something to her, but clearly hadn't meant much to him. She shouldn't feel as if her heart had been torn out of her chest and stomped on. He wasn't trying to hurt her. He was only doing what was best for both of them. She had to let go of the fantasy.

"I'll be happy to take care of Will." She glanced at the baby in question, who was still feeding himself bits of his dinner. What he hadn't thrown on the floor, that is. He looked so much like his father with his thatch of dark hair and his green eyes. When he smiled his father's smile, her heart simply turned over. This motherless little boy she already loved as much as if he'd been her own son. She wanted so desperately to be his mother. But he wasn't hers, and never would be.

"Faith…"

She rose quickly, turning her back to him as she took Lily out of her high chair. If she glanced at him she'd cry and then she'd feel like a total fool. Instead, she checked her watch. "Is that the time? I need to get Lily bathed." Settling Lily on her hip, she picked up the dishes and carried them to the sink. Still with her back to him she asked, "Are you going to bathe Will tonight or do you want me to do it?"

After a pause he said, "I'll do it."

And if she cried a little while she bathed her daughter, at least no one but she and Lily would know it.

CHAPTER NINETEEN

Two NIGHTS LATER, Faith was in the den with Will and Lily when the doorbell rang. "Who could that be?" she said aloud. Though it was technically past their bedtime, both babies were still awake. Neither had seemed at all interested in going to bed yet. And since all Faith had to look forward to was driving herself insane wondering about Brian and his date, she had welcomed their company and the distraction playing with them provided.

She put Lily in her playpen and carried Will with her to the door. She didn't trust either of them to be unsupervised around that Christmas tree. Especially not Will now that he was walking.

She opened the door to Gail and Roxy. Roxy spoke before her mother could. "Hi, Faith."

"Hi, Roxy. Hi, Gail. How nice to see you. Come on in." She shut the door behind them, glad for their company.

"We came over to bring you and Uncle Brian some sugar cookies. I baked them myself," Roxy said proudly, handing Faith a large cookie tin with a picture of a poinsettia on it.

Gail laughed and ruffled her daughter's hair. "Don't worry, I didn't have a thing to do with them. Roxy has been taking lessons from my sister. She's getting to be quite a little baker, but we have an excess of cookies at our house, so we thought we'd bring you and Brian some."

"Thank you, Roxy. I can't wait to try them. And I'll tell your uncle Brian when he gets home that you baked them."

Roxy seemed fine with that, since she was occupied making faces at Will. "I'm glad the babies are still awake. Can I play with them, Faith?"

"Absolutely." She turned to Gail. "Can you stay for a little while or do you have to get back home? I could make us some hot chocolate."

"Sounds great. I'll help you. Call us if you need us, Roxy. We'll be right in the kitchen."

"Mom," Roxy said, already involved in a rousing game of peekaboo that had both children chortling with laughter. "Like I can't handle the babies by myself? I babysit all the time now."

"Well, that put me in my place," Gail joked as she followed Faith into the kitchen.

Faith laughed. "She really is good with the kids."

"Yes, she is. She loves babysitting." Gail pried

the lid off the cookie tin Faith had just put on the drain board. "So where's Brian? Is he working?"

"No." Faith took three mugs out of the cupboard and set them down. "He went to a party."

"A Christmas party? By himself?"

"No, not by himself."

"You mean he has a date?"

"Yes." And she refused to speculate about who it was with. What did it matter? He was with another woman and what he did or who he did it with was none of Faith's business. She went to the refrigerator and got the milk carton out. "I use milk instead of water. Is that okay with you?"

"That's fine." Gail picked up a cookie and began munching on it, leaning a hip against the counter. "Does it bother you? That Brian's dating, I mean."

Bother wasn't the word. It killed her. Faith mixed chocolate into the milk before putting the mugs in the microwave and turning the timer on. "He's my boss. Why should it bother me if he has a date?"

Gail crossed her arms over her chest and tilted her head. "Oh, I don't know. Perhaps because it bothers most women if the man she's in love with dates other women?"

"I didn't say I was in love with him." Even though she was, desperately.

Gail finished the cookie and wiped her hands. "Brian may be my brother-in-law, but you're my friend. If you want to talk to me, it won't go any further. I promise, I won't tell Jay. I won't even tell Cat if you don't want me to."

"I know you wouldn't." And she did. Gail wasn't just a friend, she had become Faith's closest friend. And Faith needed to talk, even if she knew there was no answer to her problem. She sighed. "I didn't realize my feelings for Brian were so obvious. I'd hoped they weren't."

Gail smiled. "If you hadn't given it away, Brian would have. He has this certain way of looking at you—" She waved a hand in front of her face to fan herself. "Whew."

Faith couldn't help laughing a little. "Don't I wish."

"No, seriously. Cat's noticed it, too. I imagine when he looks at you that way he's pretty damn irresistible. Not only is the man hot, but he's got the Kincaid charm just oozing out of his pores. And I know all about that charm. Remember, I'm married to one of them."

"Brian has it in spades," Faith admitted. She sobered. "There's nothing going on between us, though." Just two kisses and a night she would never forget.

"Jay would undoubtedly tell me to mind my own business, but he's a man. What does he know? Why *isn't* there anything going on? And why in the hell is Brian out on a date instead of being here with you and the babies?"

"Because he doesn't feel that way about me." But oh, God, she wished he did. "He went on a date because that's what single men do." She pressed her lips together. "You're his sister-in-law. You know how he is."

"I know he has a reputation as a player. But that was before he knew he had a son. And before he met you. I won't believe he doesn't have feelings for you. I've seen him with you, Faith. I've seen how he looks at you and at Lily."

"I'm not sure what he feels. I don't think he even knows. Brian is…attracted to me. But he's not looking for a wife or a mother for his son. He doesn't want a serious relationship. With any woman. And I—I can't do anything else. I wish I could, but I can't."

"But you are in love with him, aren't you? And you love Will, too."

Faith nodded. "I love them both so much. How could I not? But it doesn't matter. Nothing's going to come of it."

Gail tapped her fingers on the drain board. "Oh, hell, this is ridiculous," she said. "Mark and Jay, who happen to know Brian better than anyone else, think he's changed. They think he's fallen for you. And Lily, too. That's why I can't understand why he's still going out with other women."

The microwave dinged and Faith took the warm mugs out. "He cares about us..I know he does, even if he doesn't realize it. But he won't let himself take the next step." Her heart heavy, she looked at her friend. "He doesn't want what I want, Gail. It's as simple as that."

"Maybe he just doesn't know what he wants," Gail said, and they brought the mugs into the other room.

Maybe, but she didn't think so. She should have quit working for him long before she ever reached this point. Except, if she were honest with herself, she'd admit that she started falling for Brian and his son from the moment she met them.

BRIAN LET HIMSELF IN the back door and stopped short when he realized the lights were on and Faith was sitting at the kitchen table. Tossing his keys on the counter, he said, "I figured you'd have gone to bed. Are the kids all right?" He pulled off his leather jacket and hung it on the back of a chair.

She bit into a cookie. "They're fine. Roxy and Gail brought these cookies by for us, if you want one. Roxy made them." Reaching for her milk glass, she sipped while watching him.

He seated himself at the table and picked a cookie for himself and took a bite.

"I didn't think you'd be back so early," she said. "Did you have a good time?"

Though she wasn't wearing her glasses, Faith wore the pair of pale blue pants and top she often slept in. They looked soft and comfortable and somehow, on Faith, sexy.

He wondered if she were wearing a bra. He was almost certain she wasn't. That made him think about what she'd do if he pulled her out of that chair and into his arms and kissed her mouth, then slipped his hands beneath that silky shirt and—

"Brian?"

Damn it, she was driving him crazy. "No, I didn't have a good time," he snapped. "Why would I be home at ten o'clock if I'd had a good time?"

"I'm sorry."

"Are you?"

She hesitated a moment before answering. "No, not really."

He hadn't thought she looked a bit sorry.

"What happened? Didn't you like your date?"

He shrugged. "She was beautiful. Hot. Available. When I took her home, she asked me up to her apartment and I'm pretty damn sure she didn't mean to offer me cookies."

"But you didn't take her up on it." She got up and put the milk back in the refrigerator before turning to face him. "Did you?"

"Obviously not." He went to her, caged her in by placing his palms down flat on the smooth, cool surface of the countertop on either side of her. "It's hard to have a good time with a woman when you spend the entire night wishing you were with another one."

Her gaze locked on his and she stared at him for a long, tense moment before she smiled, like sunshine breaking over the ocean at dawn. "If you expect me to say I'm sorry about that, think again."

He leaned in closer. Her pulse was fluttering at the base of her neck and he wanted to taste her. He laid his lips very gently on the skin just beneath her jaw. Trailed them down until he reached her now racing pulse and kissed her there, flicking his tongue slowly on her skin. He breathed in her scent until he was steeped in it, in her.

"Brian." Her voice was low, husky. Inviting.

"Faith." He said it against her skin, the smooth, creamy skin that tasted as good as it looked. He kissed his way down her chest to her nipple, which had tightened and stood out in a tempting peak beneath the thin material of her shirt. He nuzzled it. Swirled his tongue over the silky fabric and then very slowly, covered her nipple with his mouth and sucked. Gently at first, then harder.

Faith gave a strangled moan and put her hands in his hair. But she didn't push him away. She pulled him to her so he could take her breast even more firmly into his mouth. "Oh, what are you doing to me?"

"Driving you crazy," he said. "Like you've been doing to me for weeks now." He raised his head and, keeping his eyes on hers, slid his hands beneath her shirt, cupping her breasts, stroking her nipples with his fingers, tightening his fingers on them and pulling gently until she gasped.

"I don't think I can breathe."

"Let me check." He took her mouth with his, savoring her, wanting her as he filled his hands with the perfect curves of her breasts. "No, you're breathing."

He ran his hands down her body to cup her bottom and picked her up. She wrapped her legs around him and kissed him, her tongue teasing, tasting him as he'd tasted her. He rocked against her.

"I want to be inside you. Let me make love to you, Faith."

"I want you to. You know I do. But..." She stopped to kiss him, long and slow. Then drew away, licking her lips, breathing heavily. "I'm still afraid we're making a mistake."

He was hard and aching for her, wanting her more than he'd ever wanted another woman. He held her in his arms and she was soft, warm, welcoming. Beautiful. Sweet. Loving.

And if he made love to her, what then? How long would it last? Could it last?

"I don't know." He leaned his forehead against

hers and closed his eyes. "I know that at this moment, I'm not sure I care if this is a mistake."

"Once we make love there's no going back. It will change everything between us."

He kissed her again, thrusting his tongue into her mouth just as he wanted to slide himself inside her soft, welcoming body and feel her tighten around him until they both came.

She put her hands on either side of his face, her eyes so sad, nearly desperate. "Let me go, Brian. I don't think...I don't think I'm ready to take this step. Because I'm afraid if I do, it won't be a beginning. It will be the beginning of the end."

Exactly what he'd feared, as well. And nothing had changed since he first thought that. Not really.

What else could he do? He let her slide down his body. Let her walk out of his arms. Let her leave him. Alone. Aching. Adrift.

CHAPTER TWENTY

BRIAN HAD NEVER BEEN nervous walking into a jewelry store before. He didn't care for the feeling. He'd come in to buy Faith a Christmas present. Why should that make him nervous? He'd bought other women Christmas presents before, hadn't he? Sure he had.

Except Faith wasn't his lover and he was almost certain she never would be. But she was important to him—in a way no other woman ever had been. Maybe that's what was making him nervous.

"May I help you, sir?" asked a fair woman in her midfifties.

She'd waited on him when he'd come in to buy Faith her birthday present. "I hope so. I need a Christmas present for...someone."

"Weren't you in a few weeks ago? You bought the blue topaz bracelet, didn't you?"

"You have a good memory."

"Goes with the job," she said and laughed. "It was a beautiful piece and I remember you said it was a birthday present. Did your lady like it?"

His lady. Faith wasn't his lady, either. But she sure as hell wasn't simply his employee. She wasn't his lady, or his lover, or his wife— *Oh, shit*, he thought. *I'm so not going there.*

Focus, Brian. "Yeah, she liked it a lot." He smiled, remembering how her eyes had lit up when she saw the bracelet, even as she refused it. He was relieved that he'd talked her into keeping it. He'd been half convinced she wouldn't.

"Did you want something to go with the bracelet? A necklace or earrings? Or perhaps something different?" The woman gestured to the case he stood in front of.

He looked down and saw engagement rings. Wedding sets.

Diamonds everywhere. Sparkling, brilliant diamonds of every cut and size imaginable. *Diamonds are forever,* the words played in his head. He felt slightly ill.

He moved away quickly, before he completely freaked out. "Actually, I had something specific in mind, but I'm not sure you'll have it."

The clerk waited patiently but he thought he saw her hide a smile. She probably had a lot of male customers who were a little freaked over diamonds. What fun-loving bachelor wouldn't be? And Brian was definitely happy to be a bachelor. Just because he had a son didn't mean he had to go and get married. Not him. No way.

The clerk broke into his thoughts. "Tell me what you're looking for and I'll see if we can find it."

"I want a lily. On a necklace. To go with the bracelet."

"A lily pendant?"

How the hell did he know? "I guess. It's a little doodad that hangs off a necklace. Like that," he said, pointing to a large silver coin on a chain.

"That would be a pendant, all right." She tapped her lips. "Hmm. I know we have a daisy but I'm not sure about a lily. Let me check. I'll look in the back, as well, in case anything new has come in that hasn't made it out here yet. We had a delivery earlier this morning."

"It has to be a lily. Her daughter's name is Lily."

"What a lovely thought. I won't be long."

She went off and Brian stuffed his hands in his pockets and started looking in the display cases. His gaze kept returning to the engagement rings. Drawn like some kind of damn homing pigeon.

To prove to himself that diamonds didn't bother him, he walked back over to the case and stood looking down at the rings. They were pretty, he admitted. But pretty wasn't enough. A ring like that, an engagement ring, should be special, not simply pretty. Dazzling, maybe. Yeah, dazzling would be good. If he were to give a woman an engagement ring…which he didn't plan on ever doing so why the hell was he looking at the damn things?

He turned away in relief as the clerk came hurrying back. "I think we have just the perfect thing." She put a deep blue velvet tray on the counter. "I found this pendant. Someone had ordered it, then changed their mind. We hadn't put it back out yet. Which is probably a good thing or someone would have bought it, I'm sure." She placed a small piece of jewelry in the center of the tray and pushed it toward him.

"It's her," Brian said. He picked it up to look at it more closely. The charm was made of sparkling stones and shaped like a lily. It was small, dainty and beautiful. He assumed the blue gemstone was topaz, like the bracelet. The other stones were obviously diamonds.

"Exquisite, isn't it? And it's very similar to the bracelet you bought. As if it were made to go with it. Shall I bring a chain or does she have one already that you think would work with it?"

He had no idea. "Better give me a chain, too."

"I have one right here." She reached into a case behind her and pulled out a delicate silvery chain and threaded the charm through it, then dangled it in front of him.

"White gold," she said. "To match the bracelet." She laid it out on the fabric and smiled at Brian. "If she liked the bracelet, I'm sure she'll love this. Any woman would."

"How much is it? The chain and the pendant?"

"You're in luck today. We're having a pre-Christmas sale," she said and named a price that wasn't nearly as bad as he'd imagined it would be.

"Sounds good. Can you gift wrap it?"

"Of course. I'd be happy to. I'll be right back."

She went off with the jewelry and his credit card and Brian resigned himself to waiting. In his experience, *right back* to a woman generally meant anything but. This time, though, he carefully avoided the display case with the engagement rings.

What would Faith think of the necklace? He suspected she'd love it. But also that she would give him as hard a time about keeping it as she had with the bracelet…if he knew Faith. And he was beginning to think he did.

WHY HAD SHE WAITED until the last minute to shop for Brian's present? Faith asked herself for the tenth time since walking into the discount store in Port Aransas. Not only was the store a madhouse and a parking space within a mile impossible to find, but she'd had to bring both babies with her since the Mothers' Day Out program didn't meet over the holidays. Pushing a double stroller through a discount store with two overstimulated babies two days before Christmas ranked very high on her list of stupid things to do.

"They're all ugly," she told the babies, who, mercifully, had stopped shrieking. For the moment at least. "Ugly and tacky. I'm not using one of these frames. You'd think they'd have at least one decent-looking one."

"Bah," said Will.

Lily followed suit and soon they were both yelling "bah" at the top of their lungs, playing off each other as they loved to do. You wouldn't think two small children could possibly make such a racket.

"Faith, hi. Can you believe this zoo?"

She turned around to see Gail with a cart full of stuff. "Hi! It's awful, isn't it? I guess that's what we get for shopping two days before Christmas."

"Amen, sister." She squatted down in front of the kids, who had lost interest in yelling and were now trying to kick each other. "They are so cute."

"Yes, they are," Faith agreed.

She rose and asked, "Are you looking at these frames?"

"Yes. It's for Brian. And I'd really prefer one that's not hideous but apparently that's not possible to find in this place."

Gail picked up one covered in orange, black and gold plastic bees and looked at it with an expression of revulsion.

Killer bees, Faith thought. Demented killer bees. From another dimension.

"Why would anyone buy this?" Gail asked, waving it at Faith.

"They wouldn't. That's why it's been marked down to next to nothing."

"Not nearly close enough." Gail put it back and said, "Do you know Peggy's Treasures in Port Aransas? She carries picture frames. Really pretty carved wooden frames, but not so overpriced you can't afford them. I got one there for my mother's birthday."

"That sounds perfect. And best of all, I can get out of here. Thanks. I've racked my brain trying to think of something else to give him but what do you buy for a man who walks into a store, in Italy, no less, and buys himself a leather jacket and whatever else he feels like without batting an eyelash?"

"That would make it tough," Gail agreed. "So what are you giving him?"

"A picture of Will and him. He doesn't have any and this one I took of the two of them is so precious." She looked at her friend anxiously. "Do you think that's lame?"

"No, of course not. I think it's sweet. I bet he'll really like it."

"I don't know." Faith worried her lip. She'd wanted to give him something special. Something he could keep. Something personal. "I wish I could come up with an idea for another gift in addition to the picture."

Gail gave her a knowing smile. "There's always lingerie."

"Lingerie? For Brian?" Faith stared at her, wondering if she'd heard her right.

Gail gave a peal of laughter. "Not for him to wear, you goof. For you."

"Oh. Duh." Faith felt her cheeks heat. "You think I should..." Her voice trailed off.

"Seduce him," Gail supplied. "Well, why not? Since he's apparently being too stubborn to admit how he feels about you, why shouldn't you try to coax it out of him?"

Faith had a sudden vision of the two of them in the kitchen after his date. It probably wouldn't take a lot to seduce him. That night she'd still believed that making love with him would be a mistake. But now, after reliving those feelings and seeing that scene in her mind almost hourly, she wasn't so sure. "I don't know," she said slowly. "But it's a tempting idea."

Gail smiled but didn't say anything else about it. They chatted a few more minutes then said their goodbyes.

As Faith put the babies in their car seats, she thought over the conversation. Should she seduce him? And if she did, then what? She knew what was holding her back. She was afraid to risk making love with Brian because she believed he'd lose interest in her the minute she did.

Lingerie. Sexy, gorgeous lingerie that made her feel beautiful. As beautiful as she'd felt dancing in Brian's arms the night of the cruise.

What if he didn't lose interest? What if he didn't leave her? What if they made love and he realized his feelings were stronger than he'd known?

What if he actually fell in love with her?

It could happen.

Who are you kidding? she asked herself. *Brian is the ultimate commitment-phobic bachelor.* Having a son hadn't changed that. Nothing she did was likely to change it, either. The sane side of her mind knew it. Even the starry-eyed idealist knew it.

CHAPTER TWENTY-ONE

ON CHRISTMAS EVE, Faith read *The Polar Express* to the babies. Will sat in Brian's lap and Lily in her mother's. Faith had a very soothing voice, Brian thought. Melodic. Both babies were nodding off and he didn't think it would take more than a few more minutes before they could put them to bed. He could fall asleep himself if he didn't know they had to put out the gifts for Christmas morning.

He had decided to give Faith her present tonight, after the babies were asleep. Christmas morning would be all about the kids, but tonight was for him and Faith.

Which made it sound like he had romance on his mind. But he didn't. Faith and he both knew that making their relationship physical would be a mistake, and he'd decided he wasn't going to tempt fate again.

But God, he wanted to.

"Lily's out like a light," Faith said softly. "It looks like Will is, too. Why don't we meet back here after we put them down?"

"All right."

A little while later he came back to find Faith setting out some of the toys they'd bought.

"This bear is kinda ugly," he said, bending down to pick up an overstuffed brown fuzzy bear. "Tell me again why we bought it."

Faith frowned. "I think he's cute. It's called a teach me bear." She came over and touched the buckle. "To teach Will to buckle, tie and Velcro."

"Oh, yeah. Now I remember. I guess Lily's too young for that yet."

"At their ages four months makes a huge difference."

"Lily's advanced for her age, though. You can't tell when she'll be ready for the next big thing." Faith's lip quivered with suppressed laughter, but she turned away without speaking. "What? Don't you think Lily's ahead of the curve?"

Faith laughed. "Yes, but I'm prejudiced."

So was he, Brian admitted. They finished setting out the toys and Brian said, "You're not going to sleep yet, are you? Why don't we have a glass of wine?"

"That sounds good."

When he came back carrying two wineglasses and a bottle of red wine he saw that Faith had set a gaily wrapped package out on the coffee table and was sitting on the couch waiting for him. Christmas music still played softly in the background and the lights from the tree twinkled.

He set the glasses on the table and poured some wine into each one.

"Is that for me?" he asked, pointing to the package. He felt a bit like a kid on Christmas morning, wondering what she had bought him.

"Yes. I hope you like it. It's nothing much, but... Anyway, you'll see." She took a sip of her wine.

"It's pretty. Did you wrap it yourself?"

"Of course." Her cheeks dimpled. "You know I'm way too cheap to pay anyone to gift wrap my packages."

He grinned. "Just checking." He shook it. "No rattles." But something slid around in there. He pulled off the ribbon, then ripped off the paper and opened the cardboard box. Nestled in some tissue paper was a framed photograph of Will and him putting up the Christmas tree. He took it out and held it, studying it. He remembered when Faith had snapped it, at the moment Will had reached out to pat Brian's cheek. They were both laughing. He looked as happy as his son, he realized. Brian cleared his throat but he couldn't get a word out. Not without embarrassing himself.

"I know it's not much but... You don't have a picture of you with Will. I thought you might like one."

"It's incredible," he finally managed to say. "It's a great picture, Faith." He looked at her and smiled. "I'll put it on my dresser so I can remember my first Christmas with Will every time I see it."

He picked up his glass. "Let's have a toast. To our first Christmas with Will and Lily." He clinked his glass against hers, then took a sip.

Faith drank some of hers and set it down. "I should be getting to bed soon."

"Not yet. You haven't opened your present." He left the room and returned a moment later with the box from the jewelry store. He handed it to her and said, "Don't argue about it, okay? Just open it."

She stared at the gift in her hand with dismay. "I gave you a framed photograph and you gave me jewelry again, didn't you? You know you shouldn't have."

"Didn't I say don't argue?"

She looked at him and shook her head. "All right. You'll win even if I do."

Slowly, she unwrapped it and opened the red velvet lined box. She didn't touch it, just gazed at the necklace without speaking. Her head was bent and he couldn't see her expression, but her utter stillness worried him.

"It's a lily," he said, wondering if she'd recognized it. Surely she had. "Because of Lily, you know."

"I know." Her voice was low and sounded funny.

"Don't you want to try it on?" Oh, no. Did she hate it?

She finally looked at him and her eyes brimmed with tears. "Oh, Brian. It's beautiful. And so… thoughtful." Her voice was all choked up when she added, "And all I gave you was a picture."

Relieved, he realized she was crying because she was touched. She didn't hate it. "You gave me a picture of my son's and my first Christmas together. Faith, it's a present I will always treasure."

She sniffled, then got up to go to the mirror in the front hall. Brian followed her and took the necklace from her. "Here, let me do it." He stood behind her and fastened the catch, then looked at it in the mirror. It lay against her skin and sparkled, brilliant beautiful blue. "It goes with the bracelet. Those stones are blue topaz." Unable to resist, he put his hands on her shoulders and squeezed gently. "Merry Christmas, Faith."

In the mirror, their eyes met. Hers were dark brown, full of emotion. She was looking at him as if…as if he'd hung the moon. He remembered Mark's question, the night of Will's birthday asking Brian if he would be able to keep his hands to himself the next time she looked at him that way.

He knew the answer now. If he were honest with himself, he'd admit he'd known it then, too.

She turned and put her arms around his neck.

"Thank you," she whispered. She rose and touched her lips to his, then slipped her tongue inside his mouth and deepened the kiss. Slow, sweet, taunting touches of her tongue against his.

Her scent surrounded him, going to his head like a straight shot of whiskey. She felt so good in his arms. Soft, alluring, and he wanted her so damn much he hurt with it. He wanted to make love to her, to see her naked in his bed, wearing nothing but the necklace he'd just given her.

He broke the kiss and looked at her. Her eyes were dark, sensual. Her lips curved upward in a sexy promise.

"What are you doing to me?" He knew his voice was rough. He was lucky he could speak at all.

She kissed him again, small, teasing tastes, and murmured against his lips, "Driving you crazy, I hope."

"Faith, look at me." She drew back, though she kept her arms around his neck. "Are you sure this is what you want?" He searched her face for any sign of uncertainty but he saw none.

"Kiss me, Brian," she said. "And don't stop."

He took her face in his hands and obeyed, then slowly ran his fingers down her length, finally wrapping his arms around her, holding her tightly against him as he took the kiss deeper. He didn't think of mistakes or the future or even the next few moments. Only of right now, right this instant with Faith in his arms and going up in flames.

As he'd done once before, he cupped Faith's bottom and lifted her against him. She wrapped her legs around him and, as if remembering how this had ended the last time, whispered, "Yes." He walked toward his bedroom. Her arms around him, she kissed his neck as he carried her, every now and then taking a teasing little nip of his skin in her teeth. It turned him on so much he wasn't sure they'd make it to the bed.

In his bedroom, he swung her around, pressed her back against the closed door, his sex against hers. His hands roamed beneath her sweater until they cupped her sweet breasts, then returned to pull her top off and toss it aside.

He pulled back a little to see her breasts, smooth and creamy, rising out of a sexy, low-cut, black demibra. An every-man's-fantasy bra that offered those amazing breasts to him, to do everything he'd ever imagined doing to them. "Wow." He managed to breathe, but he was afraid his eyes were going to roll back in his head.

"Just so you know," she said, giving a sexy little wiggle that had her breasts threatening to spill over the small cups of the bra, "I have another present for you."

Fascinated, he couldn't take his eyes off her. "What?" he asked hoarsely.

She drew her finger across the black satin. "This. And the matching panties."

"Do I get to take this—" He pulled down the straps and lifted her breasts out. Her breasts were full, plump; her nipples tight and rosy points of bliss. "Sorry. Forgot what I was saying. A little distracted by perfection."

She laughed, a sexy gurgle.

"Do I get to take this present off of you?"

"What do you think?" she arched a brow.

In a couple of strides, he reached the bed and set her down in the center of it. He pulled his shirt over his head and dropped it on the floor. Faith put her hands behind her back to unfasten the bra. The action thrust her breasts forward in mouthwatering appeal.

Unable to resist any longer, he put a knee on the bed and bent his head to capture one of her nipples. Kissed it, licked it, suckled it until it tightened into a hard point. He subjected the other one to the same treatment while Faith speared her hands through his hair and held his head against her breast.

He wanted to go slow, to make this special for both of them, to savor it, but he didn't think he had the patience. Not now, not after waiting so long to have her. He unbuttoned and unzipped her jeans, pulled them down her legs and threw them aside revealing the promised panties. Brief, lacy strips of black that highlighted her creamy skin. He shoved his jeans down his legs along with his boxers and stepped out of them. Her eyes widened when she saw him. She looked…enthralled. Stretching a hand out, she lightly stroked the length of him. He was hard as granite and so hot for her he hoped he lasted long enough to give her the pleasure she deserved.

"I'm not using any birth control right now." She continued to fondle him. "I sure hope you have something."

"Don't worry, I'll take care of it." He pulled some condoms out of the drawer of the bedside table and tossed them on its top. She came into his arms willingly when he reached for her. He held her, kissed her, then slipped her panties down her shapely legs. He cupped her at the juncture of her thighs, slipped a finger, then two, inside her warm, moist body.

Then he laid her on her back and kissed and stroked, teased and aroused every inch of her, just as he'd been dreaming about doing night after night for months. And reality was so damn much better than imagining had ever been.

Her sexy little sounds had him going wild. "Faith, open your eyes." He wanted to see her eyes when he made love to her, watch them soften with her orgasm. Keeping his gaze on hers, he began to enter her and though she was hot and slick, he had to go slowly because she was so tight. Finally, he sheathed himself fully inside her with a heartfelt groan.

"Brian." She said his name on a long moan, lifted her hips to accept him, draw him even deeper inside her. He pushed in, pulled out as slowly as he could manage. Did it again and again. Her arms and legs wrapped around him. Increasing his rhythm, he felt her pulsate around him, heard her call his name as he said hers and then exploded, spending himself deeply in the lush welcome of her body.

A long time later, when he could move again, he raised his head and kissed her. He started to shift himself off her, but she held on. "Don't go."

"I'm squashing you." He rolled on his back and settled her on top of him. "Better?"

She smiled and touched her lips to his. "I don't think anything could be better than what just happened."

He gave her a cocky grin. "Give me a few minutes and we'll see about that."

She laughed and snuggled into him. He put up a hand to toy with her hair. It was soft, fine and incredibly silky. "Faith?"

"Hmm."

He didn't usually want to talk after sex. Sometimes he didn't even want to stick around. But with Faith, everything was different. If he hadn't felt so damn good, he might be worried about that. "Why did you change your mind about us making love?"

She didn't answer but he felt her tense. Or maybe

it was his imagination, since she relaxed against him almost immediately.

"Isn't it enough that I did change my mind? Does it really matter why?"

He had a feeling it did. But then she kissed his jaw, strung tempting little bites along it. Covered his mouth with hers and moved that lithe, naked body against his. And suddenly, he didn't give a damn why she'd changed her mind. He only knew that she was here, after he'd wanted her for so damn long, in his arms and in his bed and he intended to make love to her as many times as he could manage.

"ARE THE BABIES all right?" Brian asked from the bed late in the night.

"I didn't think you were awake." Faith slipped back into his bed, wearing Brian's T-shirt. "They're fine. Since I was awake I decided to check on them." She laughed a little. "Sometimes I go in just to listen to them breathe and watch them sleep. They're so sweet."

He wrapped her in his arms with her back to him. He felt warm, inviting. Interesting, she thought, smiling as he hardened against her. They'd already made love twice. Surely he couldn't…

"I want you again," he murmured in her ear, his voice deep and sexy. He pressed his lips against her neck, just below her ear. She started to turn around but he stopped her. "Like this." He swept his hands beneath the soft cotton to caress her breasts, then pulled the shirt up and over her head so she was naked again. "You'll like it, you'll see."

She suspected she would. She liked everything he had done to her. Everything she'd done to him. Moonlight spilled across the bed, dappling the shadows with slivers of light. She looked down and watched his clever hands toy with her breasts. Watched them slide lower and slip between her legs, touching her, arousing her. "You're magic," she told him. "Your hands, your mouth. Your body."

She turned to look over her shoulder and he captured her mouth. Then he entered her, made long, slow, exquisitely gentle love to her until she came.

When their breathing slowed, she turned around and laid her head on his chest, listening to his heartbeat. "When you asked me earlier what changed my mind…"

"You said it didn't matter why, only that you had."

She raised her head to meet his gaze. "Brian…I'm in love with you. That's why I changed my mind."

He didn't say anything. He kissed her, so tenderly she thought she'd cry. And he held her in his arms, all night long. And much later, in the early-morning hours of Christmas Day, he made love to her again. But he never spoke a word about loving her.

CHAPTER TWENTY-TWO

"LOVE THE BLING," Gail said to Faith that afternoon at Cat and Mark's house. "Christmas present?"

They were in the kitchen, ostensibly helping Cat with the cooking, but in reality she and Gail were chatting while Cat did most of the work. Roxy and Mel had taken charge of the babies when they arrived not long before and Brian had gone off with one of his brothers. Everyone else had spread out into the backyard since Mother Nature was mercifully kind this Christmas day. One of the advantages to south Texas, Faith had always thought, was the milder weather.

Bling? Faith looked at her blankly.

Gail laughed and touched the bracelet on Faith's wrist, then pointed to the necklace. "Bling. Jewelry. Were these Christmas presents? I've never seen you wear them before."

"Yes, the necklace was a Christmas present." She looked at her bracelet and smiled. "This was a birthday present."

"Do we get to guess who gave you the baubles?" Cat asked. "And come over here and let me take a closer look at them. I love jewelry."

Faith laughed and flushed but before she could speak Gail answered for her. "Brian, naturally. Who else? Don't be dense, Cat."

"I'm not dense. I said they had something going." She pointed her wooden spoon at her sister. "You were the one who said they didn't."

Faith walked over to the stove to show Cat the bracelet and necklace.

"Gorgeous," Cat said after inspecting them carefully. "The man has good taste, but that's no surprise. He's a Kincaid, after all."

"Pretty serious bling for a man to give a woman he's not involved with," Gail said. "Or did our little chat in the store change things?" She winked at Faith conspiratorially.

"I wasn't lying about that," Faith rushed to say. "We really weren't involved. At least, we weren't when he gave me the bli— jewelry."

"Aha! But you are now," Gail said and sat down at the table. "I knew it. Sit and tell us all about it. We want details. Juicy details."

Faith laughed again but she took a seat. "You're not getting them."

"Spoilsport," Cat said. "Not even a teeny-tiny detail?"

"We're embarrassing her, Cat," Gail said as Faith felt her face heat. "Don't pay any attention to my sister or me. We're just nosy."

"We were only teasing. But can't you just give us old married women something romantic to sigh about?"

"Well…okay." Thinking about it, she sighed as well. "He gave me the bracelet for my birthday. When we were on a dinner cruise of the Laguna Madre." She held her wrist out. "My birthstone is the blue topaz."

"Brian took you on a dinner cruise for your birthday?" Cat said stopping her stirring to put a hand on her hip and glare at her sister. "Why am I just now hearing this?"

"Ava told me," Gail said. "I guess she thought I'd tell you." She looked at Faith and said, "We weren't gossiping, Faith. Well, not much. But we care about you two and want to see you happy."

"Of course we do, but we really, really want to know about the necklace," Cat said. "So spill."

They were his family. Of course they were going to talk. Faith didn't mind, which was good since she expected they would talk regardless.

"Brian gave it to me last night." She touched the charm at her throat and smiled dreamily. "He said he asked for a lily specifically, for my Lily. And he wanted it to match the bracelet he'd given me."

"She's a goner," Gail said to her sister.

"Who could blame her? Talk about romantic." She sighed and shook her head. "Wait until I tell Mark. He's been convinced since Will's birthday that Brian's fallen for you."

Faith wanted to think so. But she wasn't sure. Brian had been nothing but sweet and loving to her last night and this morning. Christmas morning with him and the babies had been everything she'd dreamed it would be. Since they were up so early they'd taken Will and Lily to the sunrise service at church then come home to open the presents. The children had been precious playing with the toys; sharing that with Brian had made it even better. Then it was time to get ready for the day with Brian's family.

Before they'd left for Christmas dinner Brian had pulled her into his arms for a long, slow kiss that she was certain would have ended in bed if not for the children and needing to be at his brother's house shortly.

Yet…she couldn't put her finger on it, but something was bothering him.

"I'm so happy for you, Faith," Gail said. "And for Brian, too."

"I am, too. But—" She hesitated. Gail and Cat were her friends, but they were family to Brian.

Gail patted her arm. "Is there something wrong? Do you want to talk about it?"

"I'm still worried," she blurted out. "I'm not sure Brian feels the same way about me as I do about him."

"Translation," Cat said. "He hasn't told you he loves you yet."

"No. And I'm not sure he does."

"He's acting like he loves you," Cat said. "Maybe he just isn't quite ready to tell you."

"Maybe." Or maybe he didn't and he was wondering what he'd gotten himself into by going to bed with her.

BRIAN AND JAY had sought refuge in the open-air aviary behind the house. At the moment there weren't any birds occupying it, which suited Brian just fine. There were a bunch of people in other parts of the yard and house, but Brian and his brother had the aviary to themselves.

Jay sat on a bench, sipping a beer and watching him. "Are you going to tell me why you dragged me out here?"

Brian paced. He'd intended to spill his guts to his brother and see if he had any ideas about what he should do. But he wasn't finding it easy to broach the subject. *Hey, I just screwed up big time. In fact, last night I made the biggest mistake of my life. Even worse I'd do it again in a heartbeat.*

"They're all in the kitchen," he began. "Faith, Gail and Cat. Ava's probably in there, too. Talking."

Brooding, he took a sip of beer. "Do you know a recent study suggests women talk at least three times as much as men?"

"No, but that doesn't surprise me. I *am* married to a woman."

"There are physiological reasons for it."

"And women talking is a bad thing?"

"It could be." Very bad. Shit, for all he knew they were discussing weddings. "Depending on what they're talking about it could be…disastrous."

"I'm not a mind reader. Do you want to clue me in to what this is about?"

Brian shoved a hand through his hair. "I slept with Faith last night."

"And?" Jay said when Brian didn't continue. "Is there a problem with that?"

"Of course there's a problem." He gestured with his bottle. "I shouldn't have done it. It was a huge mistake and I knew it. I swore I wasn't going to sleep with her and then I went ahead and did it anyway."

"If you knew taking her to bed was such a mistake, why did you do it?"

Brian set down his beer, then sat on the bench beside his brother. He put his head in his hands, wishing…no, he didn't want to take back the night before. Faith in his arms, so beautiful, so responsive. "Because I wanted her. So I took her, damn the consequences."

"So it's just sex?"

"No. Yes. Damn it, I don't know what it is." He looked at Jay, who was watching him with an inscrutable expression. "Don't just sit there, tell me what I jerk I was. Tell me I shouldn't have taken advantage of her. Tell me I should never have touched her."

"You mean she didn't want to go to bed with you and you talked her into it? You seduced her?"

"No. I'm not that big a jerk." Except he was. A big, stupid-ass jerk. "She wanted to make love as much as I did. I should have resisted her, though, because I knew she'd regret it. I knew we both would. But she was so beautiful. So loving. And so sweet. God, she's so damn sweet. And I wanted her so much. I've been wanting her for weeks. Months. So last night, she kissed me and…I couldn't resist her anymore. So I took her."

Jay rubbed his forehead. "Look, Brian, I can see you're upset, but I don't see the problem."

Wasn't it obvious? "She told me she's in love with me. She'd decided to have sex because she loves me. And now she's in the kitchen with the women and for God's sake, they're probably planning the wedding by this time." He shoved both hands through his hair and stood to begin pacing again. "Now do you see the problem?"

"No."

He stopped pacing abruptly to stare at Jay. "Are you out of your freaking mind or just stupid? Did you hear what I said? Faith told me she loves me. She's not like other women. She means it. She loves me and she loves Will and now I'm going to break her heart. And she doesn't deserve that."

Jay didn't speak for a moment, but sat watching him, again with that inscrutable expression. "I can see that having a woman tell you she loves you could be a problem—"

"Thank you, Dr. Brilliant," Brian interjected.

"—if you weren't in love with her," Jay continued. "But since you are in love with Faith, I don't see why you have to break her heart."

He couldn't believe his ears. He stared at his brother for a long moment before he said, "I'm not in love with Faith. I can't be."

Jay laughed. He had the freaking gall to laugh at him. Brian had just admitted the biggest mistake of his life and asked for advice from his brother, his brother who supposedly loved him and should be there to help him, and the dumb-ass had the nerve to laugh at him.

"Brian, I hate to break it to you, but you are totally stupid in love with Faith."

"Damn it, I ought to know if I'm in love with a woman. I'm telling you, I'm not in love with Faith." He nearly shouted it. He wanted to punch Jay right in that grinning mouth of his. He wouldn't think it was so damned funny then.

"No? Do you know what you looked like when you were telling me about her? How you described her?"

Brian shot him a dirty look. In about twenty seconds he was going to give in to the urge to slug him. He could take him. Jay had undoubtedly gotten soft since he'd been married.

"Beautiful, sweet, loving." Jay shook his head. "I can't remember the rest, but take it from me, bro, you sounded one hundred percent gone over her."

"I care about Faith. That's not the same thing as being in love with her." He looked away and sighed, losing interest in punching Jay. That wouldn't make him feel any better. Probably.

"I don't think I know how to be in love. I'm pretty sure…I can't be."

"What are you going to do?"

"I don't know. I know what I should do." Break it off now, before it went any further. Being with her again would only lead to more pain for her later. But now that he'd made love to her, now that he'd held her in his arms and watched her give in to pleasure, heard her call his name when she peaked… Now that he'd been inside her and knew exactly how soft and wonderful she felt… How in the hell was he supposed to live in the same house with Faith and *not* make love to her again?

"I know what I should do," he repeated. "I'm just not sure I'm strong enough to do it."

"Here's Roxy," Jay said. "I hope that means it's time to eat? I'm starved."

Brian wasn't. Somewhere along the way he'd lost his appetite.

Roxy opened the gate and came in. "Aunt Cat says dinner's ready. She says you won't get any food unless you come in right now."

Jay ruffled her hair. "Tell her we'll be right there. Thanks for coming to get us."

"Faith said she would but I guess she forgot. She's doing something with Lily, but I put Will in his high chair, Uncle Brian. Mel's with him, so you don't have to worry."

"Thanks, Roxy."

Brian watched her run off. He hadn't seen Faith. Surely she hadn't… No, he or Jay would have seen her if she'd come to the aviary. Wouldn't they? Or had they both been too involved in talking to notice?

See, that's why men didn't talk. Look where it got them.

"Brian." Jay laid a hand on his shoulder as they started to go inside. "I realize you think you have a major problem on your hands and I haven't been much help. But don't do anything drastic. Just see how things go, okay?"

Easy enough to say. Damned hard to do.

CHAPTER TWENTY-THREE

FAITH HAD NEVER SAT through a more interminable Christmas dinner in her entire life. And she had only herself to blame. The food was good, or she assumed it was since Cat's cooking was always delicious. Simply because everything tasted like ashes to her didn't mean it did to anyone else.

She had to sit there beside Brian and talk and make sense and pretend to eat and enjoy herself, when all she wanted was to go home, hold her little girl and sob her heart out. She was such a fool. She'd known what would happen if she slept with Brian and she'd done it anyway. Convinced herself he could love her. Fooled herself into believing that he would want to make a family with her and Lily and Will.

He didn't. He'd been very sure of that. The words rang in her ears. She didn't think she'd ever stop hearing them.

Damn it, I ought to know if I'm in love with a woman. I'm telling you, I'm not in love with Faith.

Brian had been as definite as he could be. No

hesitation, no maybe about it. He didn't love Faith. And he clearly believed he never would. She hadn't waited around to hear more, but instead had turned and run before they could see her. What she'd heard had been more than enough to make her realize what a complete and utter fool she'd been.

"Are you all right?" Brian asked. "You've been awfully quiet and you've hardly touched your food."

"I'm fine," she lied. "I just have a little headache. Probably from lack of sleep." Her eyes met his. Damn it, she hadn't intended to remind him of the reason for her lack of sleep. Or herself, either.

He smiled and started to say something but she turned away and began fussing over Lily, who sat on her other side. Ava, next to Lily, said something to Faith and she responded, though she had no idea what she said. She simply couldn't bear to talk to Brian. Couldn't bear to relive the night before, even though she was certain the images were seared into her brain for life.

She'd never had a night like the one she'd spent with Brian. Had never felt so thoroughly satisfied. So thoroughly loved. But it hadn't been about love. It had been about nothing more than sex. Great sex, but sex nonetheless. Not love. Not on Brian's part.

He hadn't lied, though. He'd never said the words to her, never tried to make her think he'd intended anything more than a brief passion with her. He'd let her know he wanted her sexually. But he didn't love her.

How was she supposed to live with Brian, make love to him, when she knew he didn't love her and never would? Knowing it was just a matter of time before the fire burned out and he was no longer interested.

How could she stay in the same house with Will, knowing she'd never be his mother? Never have the right to call him her son. To hold him, love him, to raise him as her own child along with Lily.

Finally, the last piece of pie was eaten and everyone started clearing the table. Brian took her plate for her and when he came back she said, "It's been a long day for Lily. She's so restless, I think I'd better take her home. Why don't I take the car and you can get someone to run you and Will home later?"

"Will's tired, too. We'll all go home."

"He looks okay to me. Why don't you stay?"

"Because I want to go home. With you."

But I don't want you there. I'm not strong enough to do this right now. But she couldn't say that, so she smiled and went to gather the children's things and say her goodbyes.

The two-minute drive home—not home, Brian's house, she reminded herself—seemed to last forever. If they hadn't had playpens and other baby gear, they could have walked. Then she could have left without him and wouldn't be sitting in the car next to him, torturing herself with memories of the night before. She'd be sitting at Brian's house, alone, torturing herself.

Once they went inside Brian asked, "Do you want me to put Lily to bed for you? You could go lie down."

"No, of course not. I'm fine."

He searched her face but he didn't push her. "I'll put Will to bed, then."

Will held his arms out to Faith. "Mama."

She didn't say anything, she couldn't. Instead she gave Lily to Brian and took Will from him. The baby's chubby arms came around her neck and he snuggled his head against her. Afraid she'd cry, she turned her back to Brian, kissed Will's cheek and put her hand on the back of his adorable little head and whispered that she loved him.

When she turned back around she saw Brian kiss Lily's cheek before handing her back to Faith. "I think the little princess is tired. She nearly fell asleep on my shoulder in the time it took you to say good-night to Will."

"I think we're all tired," she said, and took Lily to her room.

Finally, she couldn't delay any longer. She didn't think Brian would leave this until morning. Maybe it would be better to get it over with now. He was waiting for her when she walked into the den. She stopped by the Christmas tree, the tree they'd decorated together.

He walked over and took her in his arms. She didn't resist. She wanted to kiss him. Soon enough, she'd kiss him for the last time and walk out of his life.

He kissed her. Long, slow and tender. He lifted his mouth from hers and started into her eyes. "Are you going to tell me what's wrong?"

She moved away from him, wrapping her arms around herself and stood facing the tree, not him, because she couldn't say what she had to say if she looked at him.

"This afternoon I went out to the aviary to tell you and Jay dinner was ready. I overheard something I realize you didn't intend for me to hear. But I did hear." And would never be able to forget it. She turned to him then.

"You heard me talking to Jay. Damn it! Faith, I didn't mean to hurt—"

She interrupted. "Don't, Brian. Don't try to explain. Just…don't."

Ignoring her words, he went to her and put his arms around her. For a moment she resisted, but then she let herself lean against him, her cheek against his chest. How could she still feel comforted being in his arms?

He spoke softly, over her head. "I didn't mean to

hurt you. I would never have said…what I said if I'd known you were listening."

"Why? It's how you feel. You were being honest with your brother. You're not in love with me. It's just my bad luck that I happen to be in love with you."

"Don't say that." He raised her chin up and kissed her before gazing into her eyes. "Faith, I care about you. I want to spend time with you. To make love to you. Can't that be enough for now?"

She looked up at him, wishing she were a different woman. "No. Not for me. I'm sorry, Brian. I was stupid to ever think it could be. Stupid not to realize…" Not to realize that he would never love her. She moved out of his arms. "I can't be with you again."

"So we're going to live here, be around each other all the time and never make love again? How is that going to work? I had a hard enough time keeping my hands off you before we made love."

"It won't work," she said flatly. "That's why I'm quitting."

He stared at her in disbelief. "Quitting? You're leaving? Leaving Will and me? How can you leave?"

"How can I not? Do you really think I can stay here knowing your feelings—" Her voice broke and she turned away.

"You can't quit. Will loves you. Have you thought about what this will do to him? He's lost his mother and now you're going to leave him after he's become so attached to you? He's just a baby. You can't leave him like this."

"Will has you. You're his father. He'll be all right. He'll forget me soon enough." Just as his father would.

"He won't forget. He loves you," Brian repeated stubbornly.

But Brian didn't and that said it all.

When she didn't speak, Brian said hesitantly, "Faith, I care about you."

"I know you do. But it's not enough. Will loves me, that's true. But how does Will's father feel about me?"

He hesitated, then said, "I've told you I care about you."

"Caring isn't the same as loving." She wished she could believe that if she stayed Brian might come to love her. But she didn't believe it. "Brian, it's not so much that you don't love me right now. But that you don't believe you ever will. You don't want to, do you?"

"Why do you have to analyze everything? Why can't we be together and enjoy ourselves? Do we have to map out the rest of our lives just because we went to bed together?"

And there was her answer. "I'll stay until you find someone to replace me. But that's all I can do."

"I can't believe you're doing this. At least think about what you're doing. Don't make a decision like this now, when you're upset."

"I won't change my mind, Brian. I'll start looking for my replacement tomorrow."

"Faith, don't. You're making a mistake."

"No." She shook her head. "My mistake was thinking I could live here with you and not fall in love with you and your son. My mistake was believing that if I loved you enough, you would love me, too. And my biggest mistake was going to bed with you and thinking it could mean as much to you as it did to me. But quitting? That's the only thing I've done recently that's been right."

"You're wrong, Faith. Last night wasn't just about sex for me. Last night meant something to me."

"Maybe. But it didn't mean enough." She turned and walked out of the room.

Brian stared after her. How could she leave him? How could she say she loved him one moment and plan to walk out of his life and his son's life the next?

Faith wasn't different. She was just like every other important woman in his life. Loving him hadn't stopped his sister from leaving home. And it hadn't stopped his mother from abandoning him. Love was a joke. It meant nothing, nothing more than the words.

Yeah, Faith loved him all right. Just not enough to stay.

THE VERY NEXT DAY Faith had taken Lily and moved to a hotel. Nothing Brian said had changed her mind. Of necessity, she left their furniture at the house, but she was firm that was only until she found another place to live. The following four days had been the longest of Brian's life. The nights were even longer and more intolerable. Every night after Faith fed the children, she and Lily left for the hotel. There were no dinners together, no playing with the babies or just hanging out watching TV. The feeling of loss was a sharp pain that only grew worse. The house was quiet. Empty. Lonely.

But two could play her game, he decided. In an effort to avoid Faith during the day, he went to work at Jay's clinic, putting in the new computer system. He couldn't avoid her continually, though, especially when she kept calling him to come home to interview nannies. He'd told her to screen them and then call him and he'd see the promising ones. Every stinking day she called him with another one she insisted he interview himself. So far she'd found four and he'd turned down every blessed one of them.

He was sick of interviewing nannies. He had the perfect one and Faith knew it as well as he did.

Damn it, he didn't want a new nanny. Maybe if he stonewalled long enough, Faith would get over her snit. The more he thought about it, the angrier it made him. She was all bent out of shape because Brian hadn't told her he loved her. But he'd made it clear that he cared about her. She was being ridiculous, expecting too much too soon.

His phone rang right on cue. Faith, of course. "What?" he snarled.

"I found another one. Her references are excellent. I think she might be the one for the job. Can you come interview her in an hour?"

"I'm trying to work here, Faith." And he didn't intend to hire her anyway. She could be Mary freaking Poppins and he wouldn't hire her.

"So am I. I'll expect you in an hour," she said and hung up. He stared at the phone in his hand. Damn, didn't the woman ever listen to him? Hadn't he told her he was busy? Too busy to go interview a goddamn nanny he was goddamn sure wouldn't suit him.

A little over an hour later, he stalked into the house. Faith was in the living room with the newest applicant and the babies. He could hear the women talking. But all he really saw was Faith, sitting on the couch where she belonged.

He walked in and watched the two women. Lily was playing on a pallet and Will sat in the hopeful applicant's lap. The woman was young, pretty, with dark hair and blue eyes. His son was laughing. Obviously the kid wasn't discriminating. Of course, he didn't realize the woman he thought of as his mother was leaving him.

"I'm here," he snapped. "I don't have much time so let's get started."

Faith introduced them and they shook hands, then he sat down and started firing questions at the woman. She had the right answers, he'd give her that. And she didn't seem too disconcerted by his manner, which he had cultivated specifically to scare off the prospective nannies. Maybe Faith had warned her. Faith, naturally, was frowning at him, but she held her tongue.

After a while, he'd had enough. Why was he wasting his and this woman's time? "Did Faith tell you why she was quitting?"

"No. No, she didn't." Looking puzzled, she turned to Faith. "Is it something I need to know?"

"Brian, what are you doing? That has nothing—"

He interrupted her. "Faith is leaving because she thinks I'm a lech. She doesn't want to stick around because she's afraid I'll hit on her. Which I have. And almost certainly will again."

"Brian, stop it."

He turned to Faith and gave her a cynical smile. "Why? It's the truth. You're all about truth, aren't you, Faith?"

He turned back to the nanny applicant and gave her his best lecherous smile. The woman stared at him with her mouth open, then looked at Faith. "I…see."

"I think that concludes this interview, don't you?" he said genially to the woman. He took Will from her and handed him to Faith, who was shooting death rays from her eyes. "Let me show you to the door."

When he came back a short time later the babies were nowhere to be seen. Faith was waiting for him and she looked loaded for bear. Which was just dandy with him.

"I put the children in their rooms. I thought this discussion would be better done in private."

"Works for me. What did you want to discuss?"

"As if you didn't know." She parked her hands on her hips and glared at him. "That little demonstration was completely unnecessary. You should be ashamed of yourself. If you didn't want to hire the woman you could have just told me."

"Fine. I don't want to hire her."

"Or anyone else you've interviewed. You've found something wrong with every one of them. My personal favorite, until today, that is, was the one you asked the completely esoteric computer question to and, when she didn't know the answer, you told me she was too stupid to be Will's nanny. I suppose I should just be grateful you didn't say it to her face."

"Intelligence is important in my child's caretaker."

"Give me a break. You could care less about that woman's intelligence. You don't intend to hire anyone I find for the job, do you?"

In two strides he reached her. Took her arms and jerked her to him. "I don't want another nanny, damn it. I want you." He bent his head and covered her mouth with his, feasting on her. His hands speared through her hair to tilt her head back and give him better access. He felt her response, felt her quiver in his arms and melt against him. Her tongue answered his and he wanted to consume her. Wanted to lay her down and make love to her until she screamed his name.

She shoved him away, stood breathing heavily, her lips swollen from his kiss, her hair messy from his hands. "Don't do that again."

What in the hell was he doing manhandling her like that? He'd never treated a woman that way. "I'm sorry. I didn't mean to— Damn it, Faith, I'm sorry."

"You have to hire someone else, Brian. You have to let me leave."

"It's killing me to think about you leaving."

"Why?"

He couldn't say the words. Why was she being so stubborn?

Faith sighed. "It's killing me to stay. Let me go, Brian. Just let me go."

They'd spent only one night together. Faith wanted him to commit himself to her on the basis of one night. One incredible, amazing night. It was too soon to be thinking of love. Too soon to be thinking of anything permanent. Except she was. But he still didn't believe that love was possible for him.

CHAPTER TWENTY-FOUR

THE NEXT DAY Brian went over to Ava's to work on a home network for their computers. Cole had gotten a new one for Christmas and Ava and Jack wanted to have all three computers networked and wireless. Since Cole was a computer geek, as well, he had already made a lot of headway by the time Brian got there, so it didn't take long to finish setting up the network.

Brian had brought Will along, and Ava had watched him while he and Cole worked on the computers. Faith had called and told him she was job hunting, so she wouldn't be in that morning, but she would be there that afternoon. She'd scheduled another damn interview.

He didn't want to think about her having another job. What if she decided to move out of the area entirely? What would he do then, knowing he'd never see her again? He pinched the bridge of his nose. His head was killing him and had been since the moment Faith had left, it seemed to him.

He went to tell Ava they'd finished and he had to head home.

"Let me feed you a sandwich. I have some ham and cheese," Ava said. "I know it's early, but it seems like the least I can do. Unless you need to get home."

"Not until one. Faith has another interview set up." How the hell did she keep coming up with more people? He'd surely already interviewed every damn possible nanny in Aransas City. No, in the entire county.

"So she's really quitting?"

He followed Ava into the kitchen with Will on his hip, although he had no appetite. "Yeah. As soon as I hire a new nanny." Or before that if he didn't hire one.

"Do you want her to quit, Brian?"

He put Will in the high chair someone had given Ava for when one of her numerous nieces or nephews came to visit. So far Ava and Jack hadn't heard from the adoption agency, but Ava had said it could take a while.

Brian gave Will a spoon to bang on the tray, then sat at the table and scowled at his sister. "Of course I don't want her to quit. But she's made up her mind. Hell, she's already moved out of the house. If it wasn't for Will she'd have been long gone by now."

Ava pulled out lunch meat, cheese and bread for sandwiches, then broke a slice of cheese into smaller pieces and put them on the high chair tray for Will. "Convince her to change her mind. Convince her to stay. You know you want to."

Brian watched Will happily munching on bits of cheese, banging away and babbling. Funny, he hardly noticed the noise anymore. "The only way I can change Faith's mind is to tell her I love her."

She stopped making the sandwich and looked at him. "Don't you? You certainly act as if you love her."

He put his head in his hands. He'd been so sure he knew the answer to that. But now… He looked at his sister. "I don't know. I didn't think I loved her. I didn't think I knew how to love. I've never been in love with a woman. That's not how I operate."

"In the past. But what about now?"

"Now…everything's different with Faith. Ever since she told me she's quitting, I've been going crazy. It makes me sick to think I'll never see her again. I'll never see Lily again."

"I can see that. No offense, but you look terrible."

"Thanks. I don't feel so hot, either." He couldn't sleep, he hardly ate. Every night he dreamed about Faith. Every morning he woke missing her. Was the rest of his life going to be more of the same?

"What do you want, Brian?" Ava set a ham sandwich in front of him and took the chair beside his.

What *did* he want? Hadn't he asked himself that a thousand times since she'd left? And he always came back to the simple fact that he wanted Faith.

"I want Faith to forget this stupid-ass idea that she has to leave. I want her and Lily to stay with me and Will and be happy. Together." He wanted to come home to Faith and the kids every night. He wanted to make love to her, to hold her in his arms all night long. He wanted to have more children with her.

He wanted her for always.

"Sounds a lot like love to me," Ava said. She patted his arm. "Brian, just because you've never been in love before doesn't mean you can't ever fall in love."

"I'm in love with Faith," he said, stunned at the realization.

Ava laughed. "That's what I said."

I'll be damned, he thought. He'd gone and fallen in love with Faith. He'd just been too dense to see the truth until she was gone.

"What are you going to do?"

"Do? I'm going to ask Faith to marry me. On New Year's Eve. And you, Gail, Roxy and Cat are going to help me set it up."

"I DON'T UNDERSTAND why we had to look at apartments on New Year's Eve," Faith said for the third time. "No one wants to show one today. And it's getting late. I should be getting home to the children. I mean— to Lily." Yet late as it was, somehow Gail had bullied four apartment managers into showing them apartments. This was number five.

Faith was tired. She hadn't been sleeping well since Christmas. Then yesterday Brian had cancelled the interview she'd set up and told her Ava had found a nanny for Will and she didn't need to worry about it anymore. He didn't need her help, she realized. He didn't need her.

The next thing she knew, Gail was on the phone offering to help her find an apartment. And Brian was practically shoving her out the door, offering to keep the kids so she could go with Gail.

Well, she hoped he'd be very happy with his new perfect nanny. Belinda Cramer was her name. He'd come home from Ava's full of Belinda said this and Belinda thinks that and how much Will had liked her and how great he thought she would be. He'd talked so damn much it was a miracle she hadn't punched him in that gorgeous mouth of his.

"New Year's Eve is a work day just like any other," Gail said. "But I'm off today, and next week I have to go back to work."

"I'm sorry. I didn't mean to sound ungrateful. I do appreciate you taking the time to go apartment hunting with me. It can't be very fun for you."

"Don't be silly, Faith. I'm happy to do it."

"I know I've been…cranky. I guess I'm worried."

"About finding a job? Something will turn up, I'm sure. I'll ask at my office again when I go back to work. And Jay's asking around, too."

Faith didn't answer. Even though nothing had panned out so far, she knew she would find work. It wouldn't be perfect, but she would be able to support herself and Lily. But she'd almost certainly have to put Lily back in day care. And while Lily was older now and might not get sick as often, Faith had grown accustomed to being with her all day. And with Will, she thought with a now familiar pang of despair.

She'd had the perfect job. If only she hadn't fallen in love with her boss. Her boss who hadn't fallen in love with her. Her soon to be ex-boss who had shoved her out the door this afternoon.

Finally, the manager finished showing them his last vacant apartment. Gail looked at her expectantly. "Well, what do you think?"

"I thought Aransas City was too small to have this many apartments."

"We've had a growth spurt and a building boom recently. You're lucky to have so many to choose from. Once upon a time we had only one complex."

"I'll have to think about it. I don't want to make this sort of decision on the spur of the moment."

"That's a good idea." Gail studied her a moment. "Are you having second thoughts about quitting?"

"No," she said morosely. "It's the right thing to do. Besides, Brian's already found someone else." Someone else to be Will's nanny. Someone else to be his lover?

"Then that's a good thing, isn't it?" Gail asked reasonably.

A good thing to have another woman take care of Will? Was she crazy? Another woman to see Brian every day and every night. Another woman to feed Will, bathe Will, love Will.

An even more horrible thought occurred to her. What if the new nanny didn't love Will? What if Will was just a job to her? That would be worse. The precious little boy needed a woman's love. A mother's love.

Faith bit her cheek to stop herself from yelling at her friend. Gail was trying to help. She didn't mean to be insensitive. But for God's sake, couldn't she see it was killing Faith to leave Brian and Will?

"I hope you don't mind, but I have to stop by the Scarlet Parrot on the way home," Gail said, referring to her brother Cameron's waterfront restaurant and bar. "Don't worry, I'm sure it won't take long. My sister-in-law Delilah has something she needs to show me. And then we can have a drink. It's been a long day."

Endless. Her heart sank. She wasn't in the mood to go out, even just for a drink. But she couldn't say that without sounding rude, so instead she said, "I'm not sure Brian wants to keep the kids that long. He's had them several hours now."

"Oh, pooh." Gail waved a hand in the air. "I'm

sure he's not going out until much later. You'll be back in plenty of time."

So he had a date. She'd wondered, but since he hadn't asked her to babysit Will she'd thought he might be staying home. He must have gotten someone else to look after Will. Maybe Belinda.

GAIL WENT OFF with her sister-in-law, and Faith took a seat at the bar to wait for her to come back. She let Cam talk her into a glass of wine and sat watching all the couples eating dinner and having drinks. The families with their children having an early dinner before going out to celebrate the new year. Or staying home to celebrate.

Oh, get over it. Stop moping like a loser and feeling sorry for yourself. Pull yourself together and have a little pride. But it was hard to care about pride when your heart was broken.

Just when she was beginning to think Gail was never coming back, her friend slid into the seat beside her. "I'm sorry, but Delilah was having a crisis about whether they should move away from the restaurant now that they have a baby. They live in the apartment upstairs, you know. According to Delilah, Cam won't make up his mind and she doesn't know what to do."

"I thought you said she had something to show you."

"Did I? Are you sure? I don't remember saying

that." Before Faith could respond, Gail called her brother over and ordered a glass of wine for herself. Faith resigned herself to an even longer wait. Although why she was in a hurry to get back to Brian's, she didn't know.

"Hey, Cam, do you know of any jobs available?" Gail said when he returned. "Faith is looking for something around here. She doesn't want to commute to Corpus Christi."

"I thought you were Brian Kincaid's nanny?" He slid a coaster and glass of white wine in front of his sister.

"I was. I quit." She took another sip of her wine. She was nearly finished but she didn't want to order another in case Gail finished hers quickly.

"I haven't heard of anything, but I'll keep my ears open. Let you know if I do hear something."

"What about waiting tables, Faith? Cam, don't you have a waitress job open?"

"Filled it last week. But if she doesn't work out you can have the job," he told Faith.

"Thank you." She eyed Gail's glass but it didn't look as if she'd taken even one sip out of it.

Gail plunged into a long discussion with her brother about his and Delilah's plans to move. Or not move. The fact that Cam told her to mind her own business and clearly didn't want to talk about it didn't seem to faze Gail a bit. She continued nagging him about it until he left to wait on someone else. And then when he came back she picked up the conversation again.

Faith ground her teeth and prayed Gail would finish her wine soon, but that hope was squashed like a bug on a windshield. She'd never in her life seen a woman take longer to drink one lousy glass of wine.

Gail's cell phone rang. "Sorry." She checked it and said to Faith. "I have to take this. It's the kids." She flipped open her phone and left the bar.

Mercifully, Gail came back a short time later. But she still didn't seem in any hurry to leave. Surreptitiously, Faith checked her watch. Gail's "little while" had already lasted more than an hour.

Gail took her time finishing her wine and paying the bill, and then on the way out, she stopped to chat with Ava and Jack. Faith said hello, hoping Gail would make it brief, but having a sick feeling she wouldn't.

"Gail, Faith looks like she wants to go," Ava said after ten interminable minutes of pointless chitchat.

Gail turned a surprised face to her. "Were you in a hurry to get home, Faith?"

"Not at all," Faith lied.

She thought she heard Gail giggle but since she turned back to Ava immediately, Faith couldn't be sure. Besides, why would she giggle?

Oh, my God, she thought, trying not to tap her

toe. *Why have I never realized before that Gail can be so annoying?*

Finally, they left the restaurant and Gail drove to Brian's. Just before she turned onto the street, she got out her cell phone and speed dialed a number. "Tell Roxy to meet me out front." She laughed. "Consider it my gift," she said, and hung up.

"Is Roxy sitting the kids?"

"Not exactly. She went over to help Brian out."

"But…who's staying with Will tonight if Roxy's going home?"

"I don't know. I assume Brian worked something out with someone. Maybe Mark and Cat."

"It's none of my business anyway," Faith said hastily. "Thanks for going with me today, Gail."

"Anytime." Gail leaned over and gave her an impulsive hug. "Call me tomorrow, okay?"

"Uh, sure." Her friend's eyes were suspiciously bright. Had Gail teared up? "Is something wrong, Gail?"

Roxy opened the back door and got in. "Hi, Faith."

"Hi, Roxy. How are the babies?"

"They're good. Well, they were. They're asleep now. Uncle Brian's good, too," she added and shot her mother a grin.

Gail had pulled out a tissue and was dabbing at her eyes.

"Gail, are you okay?"

"I'm fine. Just sentimental. Go on. And don't forget to call me tomorrow. Promise?"

"All right." Sentimental? Faith got out of the car and walked up the sidewalk to the front door. *That was weird.*

CHAPTER TWENTY-FIVE

FAITH WALKED INTO a room lit with a thousand candles. Candlelight and flowers, everywhere. Fragrant, beautiful lilies and roses of every color and description were scattered around the room. Vases of them. Bowls of them. Roses and lilies, her favorite flowers.

Soft music played in the background. She recognized the song. "You're Beautiful." The song that had been playing the first time Brian kissed her.

And Brian, wearing blue jeans and a dark green sweater the color of his eyes. Tall, dark and very, very sexy.

He walked up to her and handed her a single perfect white rose. "I wanted to celebrate the new year together. Dance with me?"

Stunned, she stared at him. Her head was spinning and her heart was fluttering madly and she couldn't think of a single word to say.

He took her silence as agreement and pulled her into his arms to dance. She finally found her voice. "Brian, what are you doing to me?"

He looked down at her and smiled. That wonderful, sexy, beautiful smile she'd thought she'd never see again. The smile that seemed to say he was thinking of her and only of her. "I'm romancing you, Faith."

"Brian, I can't…" Her voice trailed away. He wouldn't be cruel to her. Candles, flowers, romance. Hope burgeoned in her heart. "What—"

Frowning, he interrupted. "Work with me here, Faith. Just relax and enjoy yourself, okay?"

"Okay," she said meekly and laid her cheek against his chest. They danced in silence for a moment. "I'm not very good at relaxing and going with the flow. You know I tend to analyze everything."

"I know." He put his hand beneath her chin and lifted it up. "Analyze this." He covered her mouth with his, slipped his tongue inside and kissed her, a long, sweet, perfect kiss. "You're beautiful, Faith."

"You're very good at this," she said, finding it hard to breathe. "Romancing a woman."

"Not just any woman. I'm romancing you, Faith."

She sighed and closed her eyes, swaying with the music. She wouldn't worry or analyze or even think. She was in Brian's arms again, her head against his heart. Right now, that was enough.

"Are you hungry?" he asked her after a while. "Cat made dinner for us and brought it over. It's ready anytime."

"That was sweet of her."

"Yeah. She's a sucker for romance." He led her into the dining room, which was also bathed in candlelight. The table was beautifully set with a snowy white tablecloth, crystal and silver and a centerpiece of an exquisite bowl with a lily floating in water. The chairs were positioned invitingly close to each other. He pulled hers out and seated her, then left the room.

The music changed and she smiled a little, recognizing some of the same music that had played that night on the dinner cruise. Brian came back with a wine bottle and poured them each a glass. He picked up his and tapped it against hers. "Happy New Year, Faith."

After they toasted, he brought in their plates and set one in front of her. Tournedos of beef, with parsleyed new potatoes, green beans almondine and crusty French bread. "You remembered," she said, blinking back tears. "When I told you on the boat about the tournedos."

"I thought it was time we shared your favorite meal together. We never have."

She picked up her fork and took a bite. The meat was so tender it melted in her mouth. "This is wonderful. I can't believe you did all this." She waved a hand to encompass the room. "Everything is perfect."

"I wanted to impress you. Did it work?"

"Yes. Big-time."

He smiled. "Did you have fun with Gail today?"

She glanced at him with narrowed eyes. "Did you put her up to that? Dragging me to every apartment in town?"

"Of course. I had to get you out of the house, didn't I?" He took a bite of his own food and watched her with wickedly smiling eyes.

"And the new nanny? What about her?"

"I made her up so you'd quit making me interview nannies."

She'd known that when she'd walked in and seen what he'd done, but it still made her happy to hear it.

"I suppose you're the reason Gail was taking so long at the Scarlet Parrot." She laughed. "Oh, I wanted to strangle her. I nearly screamed."

"Yeah, she told me you were getting frustrated with her. Roxy was putting the babies to bed. Gail said she'd stall for as long as she could to make sure they were asleep when you got here."

"I thought you had a date."

He took one of her hands in his and brought it to his lips. "I haven't been able to think about another woman since you came into my life."

"You tried," she couldn't help saying.

"Yes. And it didn't work."

"I'm glad."

"So am I."

The way he looked at her had her stomach fluttering. As if he wanted to kiss her. Make love to her. As if he loved her.

But he still hadn't said the words.

She noticed he wasn't eating much. He seemed more interested in watching her. "Aren't you hungry? The food is incredible."

"For some reason I don't have much appetite. Save some room for dessert. It's chocolate mousse."

"Have I told you you're evil?"

His grin was swift and sexy. "I like to think of myself as smooth but whatever works for you." He topped off her wineglass and went to get the dessert.

Faith convinced Brian to share some of her mousse and save the other one for later. "Leave the dishes. I'll clean up tomorrow," he said, and led her back to the den. "Tonight I want to romance my woman."

His woman. She loved the sound of that. He left her to change the music again, then came back and took her in his arms for another dance. He held her close against him, next to his heart. A beautiful, lyrical voice sang about really, really loving a woman, lying helpless in her arms. *It's gonna last forever*.

She looked into his eyes. They were dark green, brilliantly alive. His lips curved upward as he gazed at her. "I picked this song for a reason. Do you want to know what that reason is?"

Only more than she wanted to breathe. She nodded, unable to speak.

"I love you, Faith. I really, really love you. So much."

And then he kissed her.

She all but melted into a puddle on the spot. She slid her arms around his neck and poured herself into his kiss. Her heart swelled with emotion. Joy and happiness and love. He eventually drew back and smiled at her, took her hand and led her to the couch where he sat beside her.

He gathered her hands together and kissed them. "Faith, there's something—" He broke off as they heard a baby crying. "That's Will." He looked put out and then laughed. "Well, that's appropriate. I'll go get him."

Lily must have heard Will because she began to cry, as well. "I'll go see about Lily." Why did children have such timing? What had he been about to say?

"Bring her back to the den," Brian said over his shoulder as he left the room.

Mystified, she did as he asked after she changed the baby. Lily was so sleepy she'd have gone back to sleep easily, but Brian seemed to want her in the den with them. When he returned, he handed Will to her and he took Lily. Will snuggled up against her, clearly sleepy, as well.

Brian cuddled Lily until her eyes closed, then put her down on the couch between them. Reaching into his pocket, he pulled out a small blue velvet box.

Faith's heart stilled and she stared at him, a smile forming. "You shouldn't give me jewelry."

"I shouldn't give this to the nanny," he agreed. "But I'm not giving the nanny jewelry. You're fired, by the way."

"You can't fire me. I already quit."

"Whatever, just as long as you know you're not working for me anymore."

"Oh, Brian," she said between tears and laughter. "This is crazy."

"Don't say anything else until I ask you." He flipped open the box to show her a gorgeous diamond ring, an old-fashioned platinum setting of pavé diamonds with a beautiful pear-shaped center stone. "Did you know that diamonds are a symbol of everlasting love?"

"Yes," she whispered, struggling for composure.

"Marry me, Faith. Marry me and be Will's mother. Let me be Lily's father. Stay with me and love me and have more children with me. Marry me soon." He leaned forward and kissed her. "Next week would be good."

She laughed through her tears and put her free hand on his cheek. "I love you so much. I'll marry you, Brian. Whenever you want."

He slid the ring onto her finger and kissed her again, long and slow and lovingly. "And now," he said as the kiss ended, "we really need to put these babies to bed."

"Why is that?" She had a feeling she knew.

"Because as much as I love them, we're going to celebrate the New Year and our engagement without children."

"Have special plans, do you?" she asked as she rose to take Will to his room.

"Very special."

"What are these special plans?" she asked him a little while later when they met in the bedroom.

He took her in his arms and smiled at her, the sexy smile that made her want to tear off her clothes and his. There was so much love in his gaze. "I plan on loving you, Faith. Now and forever."

"I love the sound of that. Forever is a very good thing," she said, and kissed him.

* * * * *

SPECIAL EDITION

LIFE, LOVE AND FAMILY

These contemporary romances will strike a chord with you as heroines juggle life and relationships on their way to true love.

New York Times *bestselling author Linda Lael Miller brings you a* BRAND-NEW *contemporary story featuring her fan-favorite McKettrick family.*

Meg McKettrick is surprised to be reunited with her high-school flame, Brad O'Ballivan. After enjoying a career as a country-and-western singer, Brad aches for a home and family…and seeing Meg again makes him realize he still loves her. But their pride manages to interfere with love…until an unexpected matchmaker gets involved.

Turn the page for a sneak preview of
THE McKETTRICK WAY
by Linda Lael Miller
On sale November 20,
wherever books are sold.

Brad shoved the truck into gear and drove to the bottom of the hill, where the road forked. Turn left, and he'd be home in five minutes. Turn right, and he was headed for Indian Rock.

He had no damn business going to Indian Rock.

He had nothing to say to Meg McKettrick, and if he never set eyes on the woman again, it would be two weeks too soon.

He turned right.

He couldn't have said why.

He just drove straight to the Dixie Dog Drive-In.

Back in the day, he and Meg used to meet at the

Dixie Dog, by tacit agreement, when either of them had been away. It had been some kind of universe thing, purely intuitive.

Passing familiar landmarks, Brad told himself he ought to turn around. The old days were gone. Things had ended badly between him and Meg anyhow, and she wasn't going to be at the Dixie Dog.

He kept driving.

He rounded a bend, and there was the Dixie Dog. Its big neon sign, a giant hot dog, was all lit up and going through its corny sequence—first it was covered in red squiggles of light, meant to suggest ketchup, and then yellow, for mustard.

Brad pulled into one of the slots next to a speaker, rolled down the truck window and ordered.

A girl roller-skated out with the order about five minutes later.

When she wheeled up to the driver's window, smiling, her eyes went wide with recognition, and she dropped the tray with a clatter.

Silently Brad swore. Damn if he hadn't forgotten he was a famous country singer.

The girl, a skinny thing wearing too much eye makeup, immediately started to cry. "I'm sorry!" she sobbed, squatting to gather up the mess.

"It's okay," Brad answered quietly, leaning to look down at her, catching a glimpse of her plastic name tag. "It's okay, Mandy. No harm done."

"I'll get you another dog and a shake right away, Mr. O'Ballivan!"

"Mandy?"

She stared up at him pitifully, sniffling. Thanks to the copious tears, most of the goop on her eyes had slid south. "Yes?"

"When you go back inside, could you not mention seeing me?"

"But you're Brad O'Ballivan!"

"Yeah," he answered, suppressing a sigh. "I know."

She rolled a little closer. "You wouldn't happen to have a picture you could autograph for me, would you?"

"Not with me," Brad answered.

"You could sign this napkin, though," Mandy said. "It's only got a little chocolate on the corner."

Brad took the paper napkin and her order pen, and scrawled his name. Handed both items back through the window.

She turned and whizzed back toward the side entrance to the Dixie Dog.

Brad waited, marveling that he hadn't considered incidents like this one before he'd decided to come back home. In retrospect, it seemed shortsighted, to say the least, but the truth was, he'd expected to be—Brad O'Ballivan.

Presently Mandy skated back out again, and this time she managed to hold on to the tray.

"I didn't tell a soul!" she whispered. "But Heather and Darlene *both* asked me why my mascara was all smeared." Efficiently she hooked the tray onto the bottom edge of the window.

Brad extended payment, but Mandy shook her head.

"The boss said it's on the house, since I dumped your first order on the ground."

He smiled. "Okay, then. Thanks."

Mandy retreated, and Brad was just reaching for the food when a bright red Blazer whipped into the space beside his. The driver's door sprang open, crashing into the metal speaker, and somebody got out in a hurry.

Something quickened inside Brad.

And in the next moment Meg McKettrick was standing practically on his running board, her blue eyes blazing.

Brad grinned. "I guess you're not over me after all," he said.

▼ Silhouette®

SPECIAL EDITION™

brings you a heartwarming
new McKettrick's story from

NEW YORK TIMES BESTSELLING AUTHOR

LINDA LAEL MILLER

THE
McKETTRICK
Way

Meg McKettrick is surprised to be reunited
with her high school flame, Brad O'Ballivan,
who has returned home to his family's
neighboring ranch. After seeing Meg again,
Brad realizes he still loves her. But the pride
of both manage to interfere with love...until
an unexpected matchmaker gets involved.

—— McKettrick Women ——

Available December wherever you buy books.

Visit Silhouette Books at www.eHarlequin.com SSEIBC24867

Get ready to meet

THREE WISE WOMEN

with stories by

DONNA BIRDSELL, LISA CHILDS

and

SUSAN CROSBY.

Don't miss these three unforgettable stories about modern-day women and the love and new lives they find on Christmas.

Look for *Three Wise Women*
Available December wherever you buy books.

HARLEQUIN®

Next™

TheNextNovel.com

HN88147

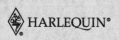

HARLEQUIN®

American ★ *Romance*®

Kate Merrill had grown up convinced
that the most attractive men were incapable
of ever settling down. Yet the harder she
resisted the superstar photographer
Tyler Nichols, the more persistent the
handsome world traveler became.
So by the time Christmas arrived, there
was only one wish on her holiday list—
that she was wrong!

LOOK FOR

THE CHRISTMAS DATE

BY

Michele Dunaway

**Available December
wherever you buy books**

www.eHarlequin.com   HAR75195

REQUEST YOUR FREE BOOKS!
2 FREE NOVELS PLUS 2 FREE GIFTS!

HARLEQUIN®

Super Romance®

Exciting, emotional, unexpected!

YES! Please send me 2 FREE Harlequin Superromance® novels and my 2 FREE gifts. After receiving them, if I don't wish to receive any more books, I can return the shipping statement marked "cancel." If I don't cancel, I will receive 6 brand-new novels every month and be billed just $4.69 per book in the U.S., or $5.24 per book in Canada, plus 25¢ shipping and handling per book and applicable taxes, if any*. That's a savings of close to 15% off the cover price! I understand that accepting the 2 free books and gifts places me under no obligation to buy anything. I can always return a shipment and cancel at any time. Even if I never buy another book from Harlequin, the two free books and gifts are mine to keep forever.   135 HDN EEX7   336 HDN EEYK

Name	(PLEASE PRINT)

Address	Apt.

City	State/Prov.	Zip/Postal Code

Signature (if under 18, a parent or guardian must sign)

Mail to the **Harlequin Reader Service®**:
IN U.S.A.: P.O. Box 1867, Buffalo, NY 14240-1867
IN CANADA: P.O. Box 609, Fort Erie, Ontario L2A 5X3

Not valid to current Harlequin Superromance subscribers.

Want to try two free books from another line?
Call 1-800-873-8635 or visit www.morefreebooks.com.

* Terms and prices subject to change without notice. NY residents add applicable sales tax. Canadian residents will be charged applicable provincial taxes and GST. This offer is limited to one order per household. All orders subject to approval. Credit or debit balances in a customer's account(s) may be offset by any other outstanding balance owed by or to the customer. Please allow 4 to 6 weeks for delivery.

Your Privacy: Harlequin is committed to protecting your privacy. Our Privacy Policy is available online at www.eHarlequin.com or upon request from the Reader Service. From time to time we make our lists of customers available to reputable firms who may have a product or service of interest to you. If you would prefer we not share your name and address, please check here. ☐

HSRO

EVERLASTING LOVE™

Every great love has a story to tell™

Martin Collins was the man
Keti Whitechapen had always loved but
just couldn't marry. But one Christmas Eve
Keti finds a dog she names Marley.
That night she has a dream about
Christmas past. And Christmas present—
and future. A future that could include the
man she's continued to love.

Look for

by

Margot Early

Available December wherever you buy books.

www.eHarlequin.com HEL65424

COMING NEXT MONTH

#1458 GOING FOR BROKE • Linda Style
Texas Hold 'Em
Jake Chandler swore he'd never return to River Bluff, Texas, after being run out of town when he was eighteen, wrongfully accused of arson. But a funeral brings him back. And Rachel Diamonte, the witness to his supposed crime, just might be the woman who keeps him here. Because when it comes to love, the stakes are high....

#1459 LOOKING FOR SOPHIE • Roz Denny Fox
Garnet Patton's life hasn't been the same since her ex-husband abducted their five-year-old daughter and left Alaska. Then Julian Cavanaugh, a detective from Atlanta, comes to town, claiming he might have some new information. Will he be able to find her daughter...and will he be able to lead Garnet back to love?

#1460 BABY MAKES THREE • Molly O'Keefe
The Mitchells of Riverview Inn
Asking for his ex-wife's help is the last thing Gabe Mitchell wants to do. But he needs a chef, and Alice is the best. Working together proves their attraction is still strong. So is the issue that drove them apart. Is this their second chance...or will infertility destroy them again?

#1461 STRANGER IN A SMALL TOWN • Margaret Watson
A Little Secret
Kat is determined to adopt Regan, her best friend's child. Only one thing stands in her way—Seth Anderson. Seth has just learned he is Regan's father, and even though he's no family man, he wants to do right by the little girl. Especially once he realizes Kat is a suspect in the investigation he's conducting.

#1462 ONE MAN TO PROTECT THEM • Suzanne Cox
He says he can protect her and the children, but how can Jayden Miller possibly trust Luke Taylor—when the public defender is clearly working for some very nasty men? With no one else in Cypress Landing to turn to, Jayden is forced to put their lives in his hands....

#1463 DOCTOR IN HER HOUSE • Amy Knupp
When Katie Salinger came back to recuperate from her latest extreme-sport adventure, she didn't expect her dad to have her childhood home up for sale. The memories tied to it are all she has left of her mom. Worse: there's an offer...from the mysterious Dr. Noah Fletcher.

HSRCNM1107